Death at
Victoria Dock

Death at Victoria Dock

A Phryne Fisher Mystery

Kerry Greenwood

Poisoned Pen
PRESS

Sourcebooks, Poisoned Pen Press and the colophon are registered trademarks of Sourcebooks, Inc.

Published by Poisoned Pen Press, an imprint of Sourcebooks
P.O. Box 4410, Naperville, Illinois 60567-4410
(630) 961-3900
sourcebooks.com

Library of Congress Cataloging-in-Publication data is on file with the publisher.

Printed and bound in The United States of America.
SB 10 9 8 7 6 5 4 3 2

To Susan Tonkin

'A Daniel come to judgement! Yea, a Daniel!
O wise young judge, how I do honour thee!'

—William Shakespeare, *The Merchant of Venice*

THANKS

To A. W. Greenwood for gunnery, love, and stories

To Stephen D'Arcy for milieu slang

To my beautiful sister Janet for lending her countenance to

Phryne Fisher

Chapter One

'What passing bells for these who die as cattle?'
Wilfred Owen,
'Anthem for Doomed Youth'

The windscreen shattered. Only then did Phryne Fisher realize that the stinging hum which she had heard above the roar of the Hispano-Suiza's engine was not the mosquito she had taken it for. The windscreen broke into a thousand shards and showered her with razor-sharp fragments. She jammed on the huge car's brakes, and it rolled to a stop. She brushed glass from her driving goggles and pulled them off.

Someone was shooting at her. Even in this year of 1928, with its notable industrial unrest and mounting fears of economic disaster, this was too much. She leaned forward and punched out the remaining windscreen with a small, hard, leather-clad fist. A bitter night. Where was she?

The Victoria Dock gates loomed. She peered through the ruined glass but could see and hear little. Two dark figures were running across the road, barely fifty feet away. One fired at her again. The bullet pinged off the wing of the car, ricocheting into the wall of the docks. They had reached the Gas Works' wall and were scaling it by the time Phryne found her Beretta and leapt from the car, sighting carefully over her arm.

She lowered her aim. Too far away and too late. The figures scrambled up over the red-brick barrier and were gone. Phryne swore, thrust the gun into her pocket and carefully removed her coat, shaking it. She then turned her attention to the car, picking out what glass she could see and sweeping with her gloved hands so it would be safe for her to continue her journey at least as far as the nearest police station. Gang wars in Melbourne? It seemed unlikely. Surely the watchman at the gate had seen something. He at least could call the cops.

It was as she turned toward the lighted gates that she realized that there had been a third actor in this drama, though he was not taking much interest in the proceedings. He was lying on the unforgiving tarmac of the dock approach road and was bleeding like a tap.

'Hell's bells!' exclaimed Phryne, wondering if there were any more gunmen lurking. 'And it was such a pleasant evening up till now. What a target I make in these lights.'

She was dressed in loose trousers, boots, cloche, a cream silk shirt and a red fox-fur coat, a distractingly fashionable figure to be falling to her knees beside a dying man under the flaring acetylene torch that lit the Victoria Dock apron.

She pulled off her coat, lest it be stained, and slid a silk-clad arm under the figure, whom she could now see was a very young man with a shock of uncut tow-coloured hair, muddied from the road. His head lolled on her shoulder; under her exploring hands his body felt broken. There was massive damage to his ribs. They were spongy under her fingers, and a hole in his neck the size of a crown piece was pumping blood.

She ripped off both gloves, rolled them, and stuffed them into the wound. A hand grasped at her arm, weakening even as it closed, and blue eyes flickered open.

'Lie still,' she urged. 'You are hurt. Someone shot you, and damn near shot me, too. Who was it?'

The head shook, the lips moved. He was clad in a workman's collarless blue shirt, and what had been a respectable grey serge suit before he had taken to dying in it. Phryne's knees were wet and grated on gravel. She shifted a little. There was a gold ring in his ear and a blue tattoo on his collarbone. A capital A in a circle.

'Do you speak English?' He mumbled in a tongue which Phryne could not even identify.

'*Tu jaspines ti Francais, mon pauv'e?*'

The dying man gave a faint laugh at the bold milieu slang produced by this stylish woman. He replied with the Parisian for 'too right.'

'*Comme de juste, Auguste.*'

He blinked, winced and said, '*J'dois clamecer.*' That was underworld for 'kick the bucket.' It was evident that he was going to die.

'*Tu parles, Charles,*' Phryne agreed.

It was a high-boned, Slavic face. The chin had never been shaved. He was paling to a tallow. His whole body was slackening into death. He drew dreadful, blood-filled breath and said quite clearly, '*Ma mère est à Riga,*' retched, and died.

Phryne held him close as blood fountained from his lungs and flooded her shirt. Then she freed a hand, closed his eyes, and laid him gently down. A foolish courtesy, she thought, as she lowered his head, cradling it in her hand, for no roughness could hurt him now. He looked heart-breakingly young—no more than seventeen.

She creaked to her feet. Where was that watchman?

There was a guard at the dock gate. He had turned his chair to face the other way, as doubtless he had been all along. He was gazing down the river as though he was momentarily expecting the *Sirius* to dock.

'Hey!' shouted Phryne. 'You there!'

He did not move. Phryne picked up her coat and went to the window. She reached in with a bloody hand and shook the guard by the shoulder.

'Wake up, cretin! There's been a murder, and the Trust won't like a corpse in front of their nice clean gates.'

The guard turned and received what he later claimed to be the shock of his life. Facing him in the blue light was a thin woman in a black hat, green eyes blazing in a face of chalk. Her pale shirt was soaked in blood. Her hand, as she clutched him, left a bloody mark on his clean shirt. Her eyes were as cold as St. Elmo's fire, and he was momentarily afraid that she was intending to bite him with those white teeth which were bared between colourless lips.

'Yes, Miss?' he faltered, drawing away from her touch.

'Call the cops. There has been a murder. I suppose that you didn't see anything?'

'Nothing.' He wound up the telephone. 'I saw nothing at all, Miss. My eyes ain't what they used to be. And it's dark.'

'On the contrary, it's light.'

'Well, I didn't see anything, anyway. Russell Street? 'Sme, Tom, at the Vic. Dock. We got a murder. Send someone down, willya? No, I ain't joking. If I was joking, you'd be laughing. Come quick.'

'You come out of there,' demanded Phryne, and he obeyed. Phryne thrust the coat into his arms.

'Hold that!' she ordered, and he clutched at the fur.

Unable to bear the cold sogginess of clotting blood on her skin, Phryne tore the silk shirt bodily away from the seam in one swift, brutal movement. The astonished Tom saw revealed blood-blotched breasts as pale as good china. She wiped her hands on the remains of the shirt and then dabbed at her body, then she tied the silky remnants into a knot and threw them down, turning her back, so he could help her into the coat. She snuggled deep into the comforting fur.

'You've got a drink, haven't you? Always a bottle of something confiscated at a dock gate. Give it to me.'

He reached into his cubicle and handed her a bottle of Napoleon brandy, part of a recently exposed smuggling attempt. He boggled as she tore out the cork and took a deep swig.

'Well now, that's better,' said Phryne. 'Suppose I go and have a look at my poor car. You'd better stay here. There might be more things abroad in the night which you shouldn't see.'

Phryne walked past the dead young man without looking at him, and climbed back into her car. It was cold and the wind was blowing straight through both Phryne and the upholstery.

I wish I had my gloves, she thought. I'd be warmer in a snowdrift! She remembered where her gloves were and decided that she did not really want them.

'Riga?' she said aloud. 'What about Riga? Centre of resistance to the Tsar, full of police informers and spies and Bolsheviks, that's what they told me in Paris. Letts had something to do with the Siege of Sidney Street. There had been a shootout and they had all been killed. Before my time, of course. I was only nine when it happened, and in Australia, but I heard about it later, in Paris. Lots of Bolsheviks in Paris.'

She could not recall anything else about Riga, except that it was the capital of Latvia. At last there came the clang of a bell, and a police car slammed to a halt in front of the Hispano-Suiza.

Two officers leapt out and approached the guard, who pointed to Phryne. Phryne pointed to the corpse.

'Blimey!' exclaimed one. 'He's been shot! Did you do this, Miss?'

Phryne choked back a laugh.

'Would I still be here if I had? Two men, running. They went over the Gas Works' wall. I was passing and they shot out my windscreen, so I stopped. I tried to help the young man, but he died.'

'Who are you, Miss?'

'My card,' said Phryne, and produced it. The policeman took it into the light to read.

'The Hon. Phryne Fisher,' he said, slowly. '221B The Esplanade, St. Kilda. Investigations. Were you investigating anything, Miss?'

'No, I was just passing. I was coming back from taking Alice Moore, the artist, home to Williamstown. We had been to dinner at the Explorers' Club. Someone shot at me and the windscreen shattered. I stopped and found this poor fellow dying.'

'Well, Miss, there ain't nothing you can do for him now. I ain't seen anyone deader for years. Perhaps you'd like to go home. My sergeant will come and see you in the morning.'

'Do you know the…dead man?'

The elder policeman looked down into the calm, white face.

'No, Miss, I ain't seen him before. Very young to have got himself into something that killed him. I suppose you didn't see anything, Tom? No? I didn't think you would have. Only man I know with one-way eyes. One day, Tom, your time will come, and then, my son, I'll be delighted to take your statement. You ain't seen him before, Miss?'

'Never.'

'Well, that's all we need tonight. These your gloves, Miss? Ah, and your, er, shirt? I see. You all right to get home?'

'I think so,' said Phryne, feeling cold and a little shaky.

'I tell you what, Miss, I'll lend you my constable here. He don't like dead bodies above half. You go home with the young lady, Collins, and make sure that she gets there all right, then ask Johnson at St. Kilda to give you a ride back into the city and some breakfast. Bitter night to be standing round the dock gates, Miss. You'll be fine with young Collins. I'll clean up here and make my report.'

Phryne started the engine, thankful that she had a self starter for use in emergencies. The great engine caught and roared. She took off the brake and allowed the car to roll back so that she could steer around the police wagon, and headed for St Kilda. The young constable, seemingly shocked by what must have been his first corpse, sat stiffly beside her.

After a ride of unexampled legality by Phryne, who could not see very well with the wind in her face, Constable Collins helped her to alight from the car, and assisted her up the steps to the front door. There he knocked an official double knock.

Mr. Butler snatched the door open as if he had been hiding behind it.

'Oh, Miss Fisher!' he exclaimed. 'An accident?'

'A murder,' observed the young officer. Phryne grabbed the policeman's arm.

'Come in and get warm, at least,' she urged. 'You have been very kind and your sergeant told you to look after me, so don't argue,' she added, handing him over to Mrs. Butler. Mrs. Butler took him into the kitchen and planted him in front of the electric fire, where he began alternatively to shiver and to steam.

Mr. Butler drew Phryne into her own parlour, which was warm and scented with roses. She gave a sigh of relief when she heard the door shut out the surprising night.

'Take the car to be fixed first thing, Mr. B.,' Phryne said, and leaned on his arm. 'Red upholstery. I want it done immediately.'

Dot came running as Phryne lowered herself into an armchair and tore off her hat.

'Miss! What happened? Can I take your coat?'

'No, not until you fetch me a clean blouse. Go and run me a very hot bath with pine salts, Dot, do.'

Dot ran upstairs and set the bath in order, poured in salts with a lavish hand, and ran down again with a velvet blouson top of Russian cut in Phryne's favourite shade of moss green. She found her mistress staring into the fire and shivering in the fur coat.

Phryne stood up and shed the coat, revealing that she was naked to the waist underneath it, and pulled on the velvet blouse, relishing the silky feel against her skin.

'Did someone attack you, Miss?' asked Dot, feeling a gentle Christian pity for the poor assailant, but worried only by the extent of the bloodstain. She hoped that Phryne hadn't killed him.

'No, Dot, I was passing the docks and someone shot out my windscreen and shot at me, too. They presumably meant to kill the young man I found lying on the pavement. It was horrible, Dot. He was wrong under my hands; the bullets had smashed his ribs. He died. He was only a boy and a pretty boy at that. You know how I feel about pretty boys—there aren't enough of them in the world as it is—we can't have people wantonly removing them. And I need new upholstery in the car. Someone is going to pay for that.'

'I think that Mr. Bert and Mr. Cec ought to know,' said Dot. 'Being the docks and all.'

'Do you? I expect that you are right.'

Phryne stared into the fire, rubbed her hands together, and noted that they were stained to the wrist with rustyred. She shuddered.

'First, a bath. I'm feeling soiled. Too much contact with cold reality, I think.'

'Should be ready by now, Miss.'

Dot followed Phryne up the stairs with a glass of port. Dot's father had sworn by port for shock.

Phryne drank the port with less respect than it deserved and threw off her clothes. Dot found that the knees of the silk trousers were wet and stained with blood and wondered what had become of Phryne's shirt. Phryne soaked and scrubbed until her pale body was as red as flame and all of the blood had been scoured off her matchless person. She sat cleaning her fingernails and listening to Dot bewailing the ruin of her clothes.

'You can't wear these trousers again, Miss, but the coat can go to the furrier tomorrow and it should be all right. I can clean your boots, I think. Are you scratched at all?'

Dot had just found some small stains inside the coat. Phryne looked down at her body. She hadn't noticed any pain.

'Now you mention it, Dot, I have got a few small glass cuts. Nothing to bother about. Just find the sticking plaster. Another item on the account,' she added, stepping out of the bath.

'Account, Miss?' Dot sounded puzzled.

'Yes, an account. Someone is going to pay it in full. Get me a nightdress and my thick gown, Dot. I'm going downstairs again. That constable must have thawed by now.'

Phryne took her place at the fire and was confronted by Mrs. Butler bearing a steaming glass of whisky toddy on a tray.

'Oh, no, Mrs. B., I really don't like toddy.'

'Try a taste, Miss. It's my mother's recipe and it's defrosting that young constable real good. We were worried about you,

Miss,' said Mrs. Butler. Phryne took the glass and tried a sip. It was warm, and Phryne was still cold. Mrs. Butler beamed.

'You drink that up, Miss. I've got some chicken broth heating at this very moment. You've had a shock—can't have you catching the megrims.'

'I don't think that we have the megrims any more, Mrs. B.'

'You watch a murder and then go to bed on an empty stomach and megrims you will have. Soup in ten minutes,' said Mrs. Butler, and nodded to her husband, who hovered nervously at the door.

'She'll be fine,' she said quietly. 'Nerves of steel. Why don't you have a sup of my toddy too? It's been a long night.'

Dot, Mrs. Butler, Mr. Butler and the young policeman all had another glass of toddy on the strength of it. It began to rain again.

Phryne sat in her parlour and thought about the young man's last words. 'My mother is in Riga.' Latvia. The Russian revolution and the Houndsditch massacre. When had that all happened? The year 9, or thereabouts.

The cuts on her body, inflicted by the flying glass, began to make themselves felt. There would certainly be a reckoning. For Phryne's scratches, the ruin of her clothes, the damage to her car, and the theft of life from a beautiful young man with a gold ring in his ear and a blue tattoo on his neck.

Chapter Two

"Zounds! I was never so bethumped with words
Since first I called my brother's father "dad"".
William Shakespeare, *King John*

Phryne seemed only to have slept for a moment when she was roused by Dot bearing a tray of Greek coffee strong enough to stand a spoon up in. Phryne dragged herself out of the seductive embrace of her feather pillows and groaned.

'What time is it?'

'Ten o'clock, Miss, and a fine spring day,' replied Dot, with what Phryne considered to be offensive cheeriness. The coffee was, however, good, and the sunlight was streaming in through the window. Phryne decided to forgive Dot and essay a little breakfast after she had taken a painfully brisk shower and rubbed herself awake.

'That nice young constable is coming at eleven, Miss, and I thought you'd prefer rolls and marmalade today.'

Phryne thought she detected a blush on her maid's cheek, but it might have been the sun. She smiled, accepted the tray, and broke and buttered her roll in amiable silence.

She had dreamed with painful sharpness about the dead young man and the sogginess of his broken body under her hands. Black coffee and cold water were taking the edge off the memory but she still felt that she owed him a life, having officiated over his death.

'What is his name, Dot? The constable, I mean.'

'Hugh, Miss…I mean Constable Collins, Miss.'

It definitely *was* a blush, no doubt of it. Phryne restrained herself from making any of the seven risqué warnings that came to mind and asked, 'How long did he stay last night?'

'Only about another hour, Miss. He was cold. That was the first body he had ever seen and he was a bit shook up. We were sitting in the kitchen. He just wanted someone to talk to.'

Dot was evidently unaware of the number of sinful activities which could take place in a kitchen. Phryne smiled affectionately.

'He was lucky to have had you to talk to, then. I thought he was a pleasant young man, too.'

And so was the dead one who rose before Phryne's eyes, blond hair darkening with spilt blood. Phryne took more coffee.

'Well, we shall see,' said Dot obscurely. 'What shall you wear today, Miss? It's a lovely day.'

'I was never so glad to see spring,' agreed Phryne. 'It was as cold as the…it was very cold last night. And today up pops the sun as though it hasn't been sulking for months. Odd climate. What does one wear to interview policemen?'

'The linen suit, Miss, and the velvet top?'

'No, find me the Chanel—no, a dress. Something light and springy—the azure one and a light wrap. That Kashmir shawl, and the silver shoes. I am feeling like a siren, today.'

Dot, who associated sirens with loud warning noises, looked askance as she found the clothes.

'You know…a mermaid. I shall go for a walk on the foreshore as soon as I can, so find the straw with the grassy ribbons. Blast! There goes the phone. I hope it isn't that idiot Jack Leonard. Did he call again last night, Dot?'

'Yes, Miss,' said Dot, emerging from the wardrobe with the hat. 'Three times.'

'I don't know why the man doesn't give up. Lord knows I haven't encouraged him. He just isn't my type.'

Phryne dressed quickly, a skill learned in many a cold Montmartre studio, and was dusting her admirable nose with *Fleurs de Riz* powder when Dot came back.

'A client, Miss, a Mr. Waddington-Forsythe. Wants to see you urgently on a private matter.'

'Did you tell him that I don't touch matrimonial work?'

'Yes, Miss. He said it isn't that.'

'Oh, well, tell him to come at two. I am going to walk by the sea today no matter what is disturbing the upper class.'

'You know him, Miss?'

'I have met him. Businessman, terribly rich, awfully boring, with a young and pretty wife who has no brains at all.'

Dot retreated. She sometimes found her mistress to be alarmingly outspoken.

Phryne surveyed herself in the glass. A thin, heart-shaped face, with grey-green eyes set wide apart, eyebrows carefully etched, a small nose, and a round, determined chin. She painted her mouth carefully, then blotted off the lipstick. She brushed her black hair hard; shiny and cut in a neat cap, two ends swinging onto her cheeks. She wondered, briefly, if she was beautiful, decided she was and blew a kiss to her reflection before going downstairs to meet Dot's nice policeman.

He was waiting for her, still looking shocked and tired, as though he had not slept. Phryne called for more coffee and sat down on the sofa, where the sun was streaming in through the window, making the patterns on the Turkish rug dance.

'Would you tell me, Miss, in your own words, what happened last night?'

Because he looked so wan, Phryne refrained from snapping that her own words were the only ones she had and obliged with a full, closely observed account of the previous evening's events. He wrote it down in his notebook, frowning heavily with conscientious effort, and shut the notebook.

'So you didn't get a look at the young man, Miss?'

'Which one?'

'The man who ran away.'

'There were two, aren't you listening? No, I did not get a good look at them and I would not know them again. All I can say is that they were not unusually tall or short, and they had the expected complement of legs and arms. Have some coffee. You don't, if you will forgive the observation, look well.'

Constable Collins drank his coffee, which was powerful, and essayed a smile.

'I admire your courage, Miss,' he said slowly. 'You didn't turn a hair.'

'Oh, yes I did, the whole thing was shocking. I don't like being shot at. And he was a very pretty young man. Has he been identified yet?'

'No, Miss. Nothing in his pockets but a handbill for the Latvian club. My chief says that I've got to find out more about them. I'm new to this, I don't know where to start.'

'You are training to be a detective, are you not?' Phryne smiled. He was rather a lamb. She could see why Dot liked him. His guileless brown eyes and frank, open countenance like a *Boy's Own* adventure hero would serve him well when he became a detective and acquired some elementary cunning.

Phryne found and lit a gasper and leaned back in her chair.

'What I think would help is, first, a little research. Find out if the club has ever had any trouble with the police—that will be in your own records. Then go along to their next public meeting with a young lady as disguise. Do you have a young lady?'

The constable looked aside, blushing slightly.

'No, Miss. Though, perhaps…I might ask…'

'An admirable idea. The Latvians are Catholic. Can you fit in? They might have prayers or some sort of service. It is always so humiliating to be standing up when everyone else is sitting down.'

'That's all right, Miss, I'm a Catholic too. I can manage that. But what if the meeting is in their language?'

'It won't be, or it wouldn't be a public meeting. Find out when the next meeting is and then you can come here and...'

'Ask Miss Williams? Do you think she would mind?'

'I'm sure she wouldn't mind being asked,' temporized Phryne, not willing to compromise Dot ahead of time. 'No woman minds being *asked*. Good. That's a start. You might look among missing sailors for the dead man.'

'Why sailors, Miss?'

The constable was evidently willing to sit at Phryne's feet and absorb her wisdom, a situation she found both novel and refreshing in a policeman.

'Did you look at him? No, never mind. He had a gold ring in his ear. Sailors get them when they cross the Line. And there was a tattoo on his neck. An A in a circle, done in blue. That must mean something. Find out what it means.'

'Could this be a Camorra, Miss?' he asked, excitedly.

'No, a Camorra is Italian and I assure you that Latvia is a long way from Italy. They simply would not know what to say to one another. Though their methods seem to be similar. It could be anything—could merely be of personal significance. Perhaps his sweetheart is called Anna. Will that do to be going on with?'

'Yes, Miss, thank you. I'll suggest the meeting to my chief, I'm sure he'll agree.'

'Who is your chief?'

'Detective-Sergeant Carroll, Miss. He has charge of a lot of things that happen on the wharves.'

'And have you been with him long?'

'Six months, Miss. He's a bit gruff. Throws things, sometimes. But he's a great thief catcher.'

'This is your first murder, isn't it, Constable?'

'Yes, Miss, and I don't know how I'll ever get used to it.'

'Take it day by day,' advised Phryne. 'Is that all you want of me? If so, I'm going for a walk.'

She stood up, directed Mr. Butler to refuse all calls, and escorted the young constable to the door.

'We shall see you soon,' she said smoothly, and accompanied him into the street. There was a cool wind blowing straight off the sea. The sun shone down. Phryne donned her straw hat, flung her shawl around her shoulders and walked across the road to the breezy foreshore, where she walked for an hour, breathing deeply, thinking of nothing at all.

She returned in time for a light salad lunch and broke the wrapping on a new notebook. She always opened a new one for each case. Being Phryne's, they were silk bound and her fountain pen contained ink of particular blackness. This notebook she headed 'Waddington-Forsythe' and looked up from her desk as Mr. Butler showed a tall, elderly man into the room.

He was thin, pale, and stooping, with weak pale eyes and a cropped head of silver hair. She put his age at sixty-five and his profession as something that took him to his office before sunrise and kept him there until dark. However, the carriage had authority and his voice was rich and deep.

'Miss Fisher? Kind of you to see me. I have a…particular problem which…I hope…you may be able…'

Phryne interrupted.

'Why not just tell me about it, eh? If I can't help, I'll not take the case. And my discretion,' she added with a touch of steel in the tone of voice, 'is absolute.'

'Oh, indeed. Well.'

There he stalled again. Phryne offered him a drink, which he accepted, complimenting her on the excellence of her whisky, and then finally unburdened his mind.

'My daughter has vanished,' he said bluntly. 'She has been missing for three days.'

'Good God, man, have you not gone to the police?'

'No,' he blushed, painfully. Phryne kept talking. If she had to wait for Mr. Waddington-Forsythe to get to the point she would be there all day, and she fancied a seat in the garden and a gin-and-tonic while the sun was still shining.

'Just nod when I reach the right scandal. She has run away with a lover? No? She has run away because of a quarrel at home? Yes. And the quarrel was about something that goes to your credit?'

The head paused, then did not nod. Phryne was good at charades.

'Not your credit, but someone's credit? Your wife? Yes.'

Phryne was glad that she had not had to enumerate all the other things which could cause young women to run away from home, such as molestation, rape, drug addiction or white slavery, and was thankful that she might be spared the usual sordid rummage through the brothels in Gertrude Street.

'So, she ran away because she had a quarrel with you about your wife? When was this?'

The stiff lips moved.

'Three nights ago—that is, Wednesday. She was violently opposed to my re-marriage, Miss Fisher. She is fourteen and… she was very fond of her mother who died when she was seven. She did not understand about Christine, and Christine did not take to her, either. They have never got on. Then on Wednesday she said that I never loved her, that I was blind as a bat, that Christine was…I cannot repeat what she said about her…'

He was about to break down and cry, Phryne saw, and a man of this type would never recover from the shame if she allowed this to happen. She slapped open the notebook and took up her pen.

'Her name, please?'

The old man pulled himself together.

'Alicia May Waddington-Forsythe. She is fourteen years old, born on the 12th of August nineteen-fourteen. I wonder if it was the war? It seems to have had a terrible effect on the world, Miss Fisher.'

Miss Fisher agreed that the Great War had had a terrible effect on the world. She thrust back memories of desolated battlefields rotting with corpses as seen when she had been an ambulance driver with Queen Alexandra's Volunteers—she had run away from school at sixteen to do so—and concentrated on her client.

'She was wearing her school uniform, and she took some things with her…my wife will know what she took. She is as concerned as I am, Miss Fisher.'

'What school does she go to?'

'The Presbyterian Ladies College.'

Phryne brightened. Her two adoptive daughters went to that school. They were both clever and observant and might have something to say about Alicia. The September holidays were almost upon them. As sources of information they would be admirable.

'Good. And at what time did she leave?'

'Five in the afternoon. She flew upstairs in a fury, then I just never saw her again. Paul…'

'Paul?'

'My son…she is his twin sister. There is supposed to be a sympathy between twins but these have been fighting since they were born, it seems. He said that she pushed past him and let herself out the back door at five and no one has seen her since.'

'What is the composition of your household, Mr. Waddington-Forsythe?'

'Just myself, Christine, Paul and three live-in servants. A small establishment. We are undertaking renovations to the house. My wife is expecting, you see, and she felt that she would like a nursery.'

The beam of paternal vanity which crossed the elderly lined face was striking.

I expect he thinks that it is a marvellous thing to sire a child at his age, Phryne commented cynically to herself. Look at the poor fish, grinning as though he's done something out-of-the-way clever. Aloud, she said, 'Quite. So there are workmen and such in and out of the house all day. Perhaps your daughter might have struck up a friendship with one of them?'

'Impossible!' declared Mr. Waddington-Forsythe. 'They are all quite common men. They could have no attraction for a girl of Alicia's refinement.'

Phryne, who had loved some uncommonly common men, especially in London and in Paris, was not minded to attempt to explain what could attract a refined girl to a sweaty, tanned, muscular labouring boy with cement in his hair. In any case she felt unequal to the task.

'I will come to your house, Mr. Waddington-Forsythe, and speak to your wife and Paul. Then perhaps I might ask the school. Who is her closest friend there?'

'Christine will know,' muttered the old man. 'I had nothing to do with them, you understand. All that young women of that age appear to be able to do in terms of social intercourse is to hide their faces and giggle.'

'Quite,' agreed Phryne, reflecting that among her multifarious faults as a maiden, giggling was not one of them. 'This afternoon, then, about four o'clock?'

'I thought that you might come back with me at once, Miss Fisher, if that would not be too inconvenient. I am very worried about Alicia.'

'Then you should call the police. Finding runaways is their job.'

'Not in this case.'

'No relatives? No one to whom she might have gone?'

'No. I have telephoned her aunt, with whom she did not get along, and she is not there. There is no one else that either Christine or myself know about. I cannot think where she is. Really, Miss Fisher, you are my last hope.'

'All right, then.' Phryne lit a gasper, observed horror on Mr. Waddington-Forsythe's countenance, and ignored it. 'She ran out of the house, pushing past her twin Paul, at five o'clock on Wednesday, and you have not seen hide nor hair since. She took some clothes and she has not gone to her aunt's. Has she any money?'

'It is quite likely that she has, now I come to think of it. She had her quarter's allowance. She can't have spent it all yet, I only gave it to her last week.'

'How much is that?'

'Ten pounds, Miss Fisher. Children are a great expense, especially girls. They must have the latest clothes and see the newest film.'

'Did she go to many films?' Phryne was trying to get a grasp on the character of the girl. So far she was shadowy in the extreme.

'No, actually, she didn't. Spent a lot of time at church. St. Peter's, Eastern Hill, you know. She sang in the choir and was very active in the Girls' Brigade and the Band of Hope. Always went to both services on Sunday. Christine thinks that it is a phase. Wanted to enter a sisterhood a few months ago. I put my foot down about that.'

'Which sisterhood?'

'The Anglican Sisters of Charity, in Eltham, or some such place. I daresay that they do a lot of good, and it's an excellent way to dispose of surplus women—better than having them meddling about in nursing or trying to go into parliament—but not for my daughter. I expect her to make a good marriage.'

'Did you enquire of the sisterhood? Was Alicia there?'

'Pack of scheming women,' commented Mr. Waddington-Forsythe. 'Said that "Miss Waddington-Forsythe was not there." When I tried to persuade the confounded Mother Superior, or whatever idiotic title they give themselves, to tell me where she might be she said that it was time for matins and rang off. But Alicia was happy with the sisters. Or so I believe.'

'So she might still go there,' said Phryne, very gently because she was restraining an urge to bean this Victorian relic with a lampstand. Mr. Waddington-Forsythe scowled.

'Yes, it's possible. I'm coming to you, Miss Fisher, because the detective who was my first choice said that you could manage this job under the constraints which I have been obliged to apply to it. He refused to touch it and said that only the police can catch runaways, and if the Anglican Sisterhood was involved then he had an urgent appointment in China. Damn the man! I believe that he was afraid of them.'

Phryne butted out her cigarette and lit another one, which she did not want, solely to annoy her client. What an unprepossessing thing, she thought, to see the upjumped social-climbing middle class in terror of its position. Poor girl. Religious mania may have seemed positively sane by comparison.

'All right. I'll come with you now.'

'You'll take the case?'

'One week. If I don't find her within the week, Mr. Waddington-Forsythe, then you will hand the case over to the police, with my notes as to the progress of my investigations. That is my constraint. Do you accept?'

'I accept,' he said, promptly. 'My car is outside, Miss Fisher.'

◇◇◇

The ride, in a chauffeured Bentley, was comfortable. Mr. Waddington-Forsythe did not speak. The chauffeur handed Phryne out in the grounds of an extensive Victorian mansion. Three storeys, plus a series of attics; pillared portico and every window gleaming. One side of the house was disfigured by the skeletal beginnings of a new wing, evidently to be built in the most modern style, matching the existing structure in no respect whatsoever. It was curved, like the wing of a bird, and seemed to be constructed mostly of concrete. Several workmen were in view, doing important things with plumb lines.

'Renovations? I'd say that you were building a new house, Mr. Waddington-Forsythe.' This name was going to be a problem, Phryne thought. Perhaps she could get away with calling him 'sir.' He might like that and it would cut down the wear and tear on her vocal cords.

'Yes, Miss Fisher, it is an entirely original design by the most fashionable architect. Sir Adrian Griffith was kind enough to say that he found it most striking.'

Phryne agreed. Striking it certainly was. And if the new wife wanted to make an eyesore out of an honest old house, it was not her business. She felt about modern art as she felt about Baroque additions to Gothic churches. The only time that it looked good was in a building built for it.

A butler of some magnificence opened the front door for the master and led Phryne into an opulent hall, high-ceilinged and gilded, to which someone had added a black glass floor and a hatstand composed of lengths of chromium pipe. Phryne gave up her hat and wrap and was taken into an entirely modern parlour to meet the lady of the house.

Christine Waddington-Forsythe was twenty-five at the most and very pretty, in a large-eyed, frightened-doe way. She was quite evidently about five months pregnant and was dressed in a loose, white wrapper. Her long fingers pleated the edge of this nervously. Sitting beside her on the copper sofa was a scowling boy. He was extravagantly beautiful, having curly blond hair, blue eyes, and a face which Raphael, or perhaps Botticelli, would have sold their grandmothers to paint. He struck Phryne still in her steps and silenced her in the middle of her polite greeting with a loud, 'Well, are you going to find her?'

'I hope so, indeed. My name is Phryne Fisher. Are you Paul?'

'The Honourable Phryne Fisher,' Mr. Waddington-Forsythe put in his oar. The boy's angelic face creased further.

'Well, Miss Honourable Phryne Fisher, are you going to find her?'

'I shall try.'

Phryne sat down collectedly and lit a gasper. Mrs. Waddington-Forsythe looked ready to faint, but the boy suddenly grinned and got up, unfolding an unexpected length of leg clad in tennis flannels.

'I'll find you an ashtray,' he offered.

'Show me her room,' suggested Phryne, following up her advantage. The boy blanched, steadied himself, and looked at his stepmother.

'I'll take Miss Fisher up, Paul,' she said, easily. Her husband laid a hand on her arm.

'No, no, m'dear, you must not fatigue yourself. Paul will do very well.'

With an agonized backward glance, Paul led the way up the stairs, along a carpeted corridor and indicated a closed door.

'In here?'

He nodded, swallowing hard.

'Just wait for me, then.'

Phryne opened the door and entered a small but well-ap-
pointed room. There was a wardrobe with school uniforms and
Sunday dresses, a sufficiency of underclothes and sports clothes
and a selection of shoes. The girl had not cared particularly for
her appearance. Phryne found no make-up, not even a clandes-
tine pot of rouge, powder, or a hidden tube of lipstick. There
were religious prints on the walls, the largest being a Grünewald
crucifixion, an odd adornment for a girl's room. Phryne stared
for a while at the painting, which hung directly below the
maidenly white bed, presumably so that Alicia could see it all
the time. Green, tortured, leprous, twisted in agony, the fingers
and toes curled around the piercing nails, it was gruesome; more
gruesome even than real death. The painter had inflicted on this
suffering, crippled body all the plagues of the world. Doubtless as
a metaphor for all sins, Phryne thought, shuddering as though a
goose had danced a whole quadrille upon her grave. She turned
to the books.

All works of devotion: a bible, a prayer book. Phryne held
them up by the spine, one by one, and shook them, garnering
a harvest of little cards, devotional stamps and pressed flowers. Nothing in the girl's own writing but a copy of the Ten
Commandments, which had been printed on a card, doubtless
for easy reference. Next to 'Honour thy Father and thy Mother'
she had written, 'so difficult. I don't want to fall into sin but I
can't'. The *can't* had been underscored so hard that the pencil
had torn through the surface of the paper.

No letters, no diary. Her school books revealed that she
was a middle-of-the-road student with an interest in Latin and
Music, and it appeared that she played chess. Some chess problems had been carefully copied out and solved, one with three
exclamation marks.

Her violin was still in its case. Phryne took it out and plucked
a string: mellow, delicate, sad. It was an expensive instrument
and she replaced it with care, having searched the case.

She heard a thud in the corridor and opened the door. The
exquisite Paul had heard the voice of the violin and had fainted.

Phryne left him where he was and continued her search. She tapped the walls, looking for a hiding place. A girl of this religiosity would certainly have kept a diary, if only to remind herself of her righteous struggle against sin. The walls were solid Victorian panelling, the floor was covered by a carpet which had been nailed down all round, and there was no space in the win-dowseat, which was full of woollens. Phryne took each jumper out and shook it, but there was nothing there. She must have taken her diary with her. So. Paul should be recovering and she went out to see how he was.

He was sitting groggily on the floor and she extended a strong hand to pull him to his feet. He came up swiftly into her arms and for a moment their faces were very close. The rosebud mouth opened and moistened; Phryne thought that he was going to kiss her, and wondered what she should do.

Fortunately for her virtue, the moment passed. The body which had clung close released itself; Phryne wondered if she had been imagining things. Could there be such a depth of sensuality in a young boy?

'There. A little overcome, eh? Were you very fond of your sister?' Wrong question. He stiffened and pulled away from her embrace.

'No. Interfering little busybody, always poking her nose in, with her damned religion. Thought she was better than anyone, she did. But I don't like her being missing.'

He led the way down the stairs, where Phyne conducted a brief conversation with Christine, who spoke in a weakening whisper.

'She took her swimming bag and a change of clothes. That's all that I could find missing.'

'And you have no idea where she has gone?'

'Not unless she is with the sisterhood. She had enough money to get to Eltham, but they say she isn't there.'

'Are you worried about her?'

'Of course.'

'Was she the sort of girl who was, well, easily deceived? Would she get into a stranger's car, for instance?'

'No. Not if it was a man. She was very…shy.'

'She didn't like boys?'

'Not at all.'

'And who was her best friend at school?'

'I'm sure I don't know, Miss Fisher. She never confided in me.'

'And what about her diary?'

The gentle eyes, lids drooping with weariness, suddenly flashed. Phryne had Mrs. Waddington-Forsythe's full attention.

'Her diary? Oh yes. I suppose she took it with her. Now I really must go and lie down, Miss Fisher. My doctor says that I must rest for three hours every afternoon. If you will excuse me?'

Phryne watched her glide listlessly away, and faced the old man and the boy. They were both staring after the retreating drapery.

'I'll report in a week,' said Phryne. She walked out of the house, and was driven with care back to her own house.

Chapter Three

'The boy by my side, shot through the head,
lay…soaking my shoulder, for half an hour…
can you photograph the crimson-hot iron as
it cools from the smelting? That is what Jones'
blood looked like, and felt like. My senses are
charred. I shall feel it as soon as I dare, but
now I must not.'

Wilfred Owen, Diary: May 1918

Phryne was possessed of sudden disgust. She told Dot to find
Bert and Cec and ask them to dinner, then ran up the stairs and
flung herself into a padded chair in front of the window which
looked straight out to sea. She poured a small whisky and lit
a cigarette, for she could still smell blood on her breast, and it
worried her.

I must be going mad, she chided herself. I've seen lots of
dead men. And I do not smell of blood. It is washed off me and
I am wearing different clothes. I must take hold of myself. Ah.
Here are the books which Dot has obtained from the library. I
shall drink this whisky and then another and I shall feel better.

Having given herself suitable orders, she opened the first book
and began to read as much as was known, which was not much,
about Latvia, Lithuania, Russia, and the Revolution.

After two hours of concentrated study, the situation was still unclear and Phryne decided to stop and review her notes.

Latvia appeared to have been fought over and shared out between all her neighbours. Poland, Sweden and Russia had all conquered it in turn and like Gaul it had been divided into three parts: Livonia, Courland, and Latgale on the border of Russia—an unsafe place to be. She was reminded of a comment about the constant war in Poland. 'Well, if you pitch your tent in the middle of Piccadilly you are going to get run over.' The Baltic had been troubled since written history began and seemed to 'produce more history than they could consume, locally' which might have been the reason that they had continually exported trouble.

Nasty things had happened to Latvia during the Great War, and nastier when the Revolution had transformed October forever. Lithuania was forever fighting with Poland about who owned Vilna. It was closest to Russia.

It appeared to be Catholic, as most of the Baltic coast was, which would not please the Bolsheviks. In the Great War it had been occupied by Germany and then Russia; the Soviets had reluctantly accepted the independence of the Baltic States in 1920. Litvinov had signed a non-aggression pact with them. Nothing more was apparent from the books, and Phryne reviewed the early history. The Swedes and Teutons had been driven out by the famous Alexander Nevsky in the battle of the Raven's Rock. The name pleased Phryne, and she folded up the notes and poured herself another small whisky. Where to find some modern history? It did not seem to have been written down in these sober tomes from the public library.

She thought of her friends, Vera and Joseph Wilson, who would certainly know what was happening in Latvia. They were red-raggers of the deepest dye, and very good company when they could be induced to talk about anything other than politics. Vera kept a political salon of the Trotskyite persuasion and Joseph sculpted. Or did he write poetry? Something artistic, anyway.

Phryne called the Wilsons, who were home, and asked herself to supper that night. It appeared that a lot of company was expected. She did this in cold earnest, having attended Wilson suppers before. It was a measure of her dedication that she did not flinch.

◇◇◇

Dinner with Bert and Cec was always amusing, especially as Mrs. Butler liked them and made unusual efforts with the food.

'Who was on the gates, Miss?' asked Bert, and snorted when Phryne described the watchman.

'That's Tom. He'd never notice a murder. Might get him into trouble. He only notices some poor coot who's trying to take out a tin or two of peaches or a bar of chocolate. He loves pinching them. But anything big and nasty, Tom's not your man. You musta scared him out of ten years' growth, Miss.'

Bert chuckled and accepted another roasted potato. The saddle of lamb was perfectly cooked and had all the traditional accompaniments, except Yorkshire pudding, which Phryne did not like, having had a surfeit of it in early childhood.

'Yair,' agreed Cec. 'He wouldn't be no help. What was the tattoo, Miss?'

Phryne drew it on the tablecloth with her finger. Bert whistled.

'You know it?'

'Anarchists,' said Bert, consulting Cec with a glance. 'Anarchists, they have that tattoo. Bad men, Miss.'

'Are there anarchists on the wharf?'

'Yair, reckon. We got all sorts, Miss. Lot of 'em are Wobblies, and there's the comrades, then the Stalinists and the Trotskyites.'

'Which are you, Bert?'

'I'm just a commo, Miss. I don't care about what's happening in Russia. I reckon with a history like theirs they won't make any better fist of communism than they did of feudalism. Big, strange place, Russia. And I don't like their leaders. Since Lenin died and the Tsar was assassinated it's all gone down. Pity. The Great Social Experiment, it is. But with a system which still uses the army to crush the masses, I don't hold out much hope for it. Here is where we need the Revolution, Miss. Can I have some more lamb?'

Mr. Butler loaded Bert's plate. Cec put in, quietly, 'If you are going to be mixing with the anarchists, Miss, I reckon you'd better take us along. I hear that they have guns. Why not let Bert and me go to ground and see if we can pick up a whisper? They used to rob banks,' he added, 'and you can't just go into Markillies', Miss, can you, and have a beer with the boys.'

'No, I can't, and that is a generous offer, but I would not like to send you into danger,' protested Phryne. 'The Revolution needs you—and I need you, too. And Alice needs Cec.'

'Yair,' agreed Bert. 'And my landlady needs me. Another thing. Come September the tenth the wharves will be dead. No one will report for work. So we'd better get cracking.'

'Why will no one report for work on the tenth?'

'Beeby award,' growled Bert. 'They're trying to reorganize the docks. Want two pick-ups a day. That means that if you don't get a job you have to wait for the late pick-up. Man could waste a lifetime hanging around. They want to lower our wages and cut down conditions and grind us into the dirt, so they either change the award or we go out, and we stay out.'

'Well it's the first of September today. Better, as you say, get cracking. I've told you all I know, which is very little. Go any-where, spend any money, but I want these bastards. They shot my car and they tried to shoot me and they killed a beautiful young man and he died in my arms and I cannot forgive them. Understood? Any news, ring me. I've got another job, but this is of the first importance.'

Bert nodded, with his mouth full. Cec accepted ten quid on account and stowed the notes away.

'Tell me all you know about the anarchists,' she ordered.

Bert swallowed, shot a glance at Cec, and began, 'They were involved in the fight against the Tsar in Russia, that's where they learned their bad habits. They blew up Tsar Alexander, the last Tsar's father. They believe in nothing; that if society was free, without laws or police or gaols, then it would be virtuous.

Meself, I can't see it. And they act like ordinary gangsters. In London in 1909 and 1910, they staged a few bank robberies and a wages snatch which went wrong. Political consciousness ain't no replacement for good planning, Miss. They shot their way out, killing children and women, which real revolutionaries would never do, then finally got caught in the Siege of Sidney Street—you must have heard of it.'

Phryne nodded. She had been in Australia and a child at the time but some news had filtered through.

'They poured bullets into the house, and the anarchists poured 'em out. Eventually the house caught fire and they were all killed.'

'So that was the end of them?'

'No, Miss! You can't kill off anarchists like that. There were more of them. Some had been in Paris and some weren't in the house. Peter the Painter was one. There was…'

Bert broke off and took some more potato.

'There was…?' prompted Phryne. Cec grinned.

'It's a secret, Miss, but you already know, I expect. We heard that some of them anarchists came to Melbourne, to work on the wharf. Peter the Painter was supposed to be one of 'em. But there's a lot of Balts on the docks and he could be any one of 'em. I don't suppose he looks like his police photo any more and I don't think they had fingerprints when he was captured last. Anarchists were supposed to have something to do with two bank robberies this year, but as I said, we don't know that, it's just rumour. There are more stories on the wharf than Moss Trooper could jump over.'

'I see. Well, that is very interesting and if you have finished, Mrs. Butler will bring in dessert. You will be careful, Bert, Cec, won't you? I'd hate anything to happen to you.

'The anarchists. I want to know who they are, where they meet, and most especially I want to know who the young man was and why they shot him. Get me whatever you can.'

'What are you going to do, Miss?' asked Cec, accepting a cup of coffee and a small port.

Phryne sipped port and smiled.

'I am going to supper with the Wilsons in Brunswick, whence you shall drive me in the taxi, and wait, if you please. That is the fashionable face of communism; I might pick up something. Probably fleas, if Vera still has that verminous Spanish guitarist infesting the place. Are you with me?'

Bert and Cec raised their glasses. Bert was short and stout. Cec was tall and lanky. Between them, there was nothing that they could not reach.

'We're with you,' agreed Bert. 'And maybe we won't get shot at so much this time. A man begins to feel like a target. Cheers,' and he downed the glass of very good port.

◇◇◇

Phryne dressed for the Wilsons. A peasant skirt, bias-cut and braided, which waved around her ankles; a heavily embroidered tunic in fine wool with flowing white lawn sleeves beneath it, and a boxy little hat with attached scarf. She wore soft red Russian leather boots and took a large handbag, stuffing into it a lot of pound notes—Vera always had causes to be financed—her little gun and a new packet of cigarettes. Not even for revenge was she going to smoke Joseph's frightful revolutionary South American cigars.

Dot looked in as she was about to leave.

'Got everything, Miss? And is this dangerous? Shall I wait up for you?'

'No, just the usual Wilson supper. Don't wait up. See you later.' She waved at Dot as she passed and descended the stairs at a run. Bert and Cec were waiting for her in the salon and they went out to the cab, with no comment except for a brief, 'Crikey!' from Bert in relation to her costume.

The drive to Brunswick was comfortable and Phryne recruited her strength by dozing in the back seat. She disliked the Wilsons' parties intensely, not because of any fault in the Wilsons, who were darlings, but because of their habit of cramming their very small house with every red-ragger, painter, sculptor and poet they could find, and expecting them to perform all at once. It had led to some memorable evenings and quite a lot of fights.

Phryne recalled the expression of a Catalan nobleman who had just had a certain suggestion put to him by a very advanced poet of the body-urge and laughed herself awake.

Vera was standing at the top of the stairs as Phryne toiled up two flights, tripping over pails and a perambulator. She was a tall woman with the limbs of a Valkyrie and the general aspect of a rather vague and benevolent Brunnhilde. Her long blonde hair was always plaited into two braids coiled over her ears and she had a regrettable tendency to wear smocks—in fact, she was wearing one now. It had hollyhocks embroidered on it.

The noise from the rooms behind was terrific.

'Hello, Vera. Nice to see you again! How's the Revolution?' yelled Phryne above the babble of many voices and the strumming of what was probably a lute. Vera beamed.

'Phryne, my dear! We have lots of people you must meet. Do come in, can I get you a drink?'

Phryne considered. She was quite full and it seemed a terrible insult to that fine old British Empire Oporto nectar to follow it with any of the nauseous fluids likely to be lurking on Vera's premises under the name of 'drink.'

'Just some water,' she trilled, lifting her voice to carry. Vera fought her way back through the crowd with a beer glass full of what was probably water, or what passed for water in Brunswick. Someone seized her by the ankle and she looked down.

'Poetry is a function of rebellion,' growled a black beard. 'I will now recite the poem I wrote on the occasion of Lenin's death.'

'Later,' promised Phryne, and fled, stumbling over several people of indeterminate sex who were entwined so closely that she could only tell that there were three of them by the heads.

She cannoned straight into Vera's back, and was saved from falling by a strong hand which dragged her up. She looked into a rather lined and weary Slavic face, with dark blue eyes and greying brown hair. He smiled sweetly and Vera turned around.

'Oh, Phryne, there you are. This is Peter Smith, he's the one to tell you all about the Lithuanian situation. Knows everyone. Peter, this is Phryne Fisher, an old friend of mine.'

Peter Smith, in whose name Phryne did not for an instant believe, lifted the hand he held to his lips and kissed it.

'Miss Fisher,' he said. His voice was deep and very attractive. 'I am honoured to meet so famous a detective. Is it an investigation which brings you here?'

Phryne considered. Some part of the truth seemed necessary.

'Someone tried to shoot me,' she said bluntly. 'I dislike being shot at.'

'I can understand that,' agreed Peter Smith, guiding Phryne around a large table loaded with books and oranges. 'Would you like an orange? The fruit boat at 5 North today had a loading accident.'

Phryne took one and leaned against the table as it appeared that she was not going to get any further into the room. This was a personable man, she thought, a little stocky, perhaps, but beautifully muscled. His stance was weary and his air cautious.

'Who shot at you?' he asked, with every appearance of really wanting to know.

'Anarchists, I believe.' Phryne peeled the orange assiduously. 'Outside Victoria Dock gates. Last night,' she added. 'The police tell me that they were anarchists. So I want to know more about them. Why, for instance, did they want me dead?'

'That does not sound like them,' said Peter, quietly. 'What had you done?'

'Nothing, I was just driving past on a public road when the windscreen of my car shattered.'

'Did you see them?'

'Yes,' said Phryne, splitting the fruit neatly down the middle. 'I saw them.'

She omitted to mention that what she had seen was two shapes which presumably were men and which she would never know again.

'This is most disturbing, Miss Fisher...Fisher?'

'That is my name. Tell me about Latvia and about anarchists.'

'Vera said Lithuania.'

'Latvia,' said Phryne through a mouthful of orange. 'This is a really good orange. Do you work on the wharf?'

'Yes. Latvia, well, it has been many years since I have been there. What is happening in Latvia I have only heard from the exiles, and exiles cannot be depended upon.'

'Nevertheless.'

'Litvinov signed a non-aggression pact.'

'In 1920.'

'So. You have been reading. But Russia has always coveted the Baltic states, because the Baltic Sea has warm water ports. Lenin died in 1924 and that has been the ruin of Russia. Now that Stalin is in control, I fear that Latvia will not long keep her independence. Already there are spies of the Bolsheviks in all the Baltic states, and there have been arrests, and now that the forced communalization of the country is happening in Russia, Latvia cannot be long untouched. There will be massacres and much unhappiness and more and more of the people will flee. More will come here, perhaps, because it is better to plot revolution in a country a long way from the OGPU.'

'And who are they?'

'They used to be the Cheka. They are the secret arm of the Russian state. Some of their agents were Tsarist spies. It is not so long since the Tsar fell, you know.'

'Indeed. And are there many anarchists here?'

'Not only anarchists and Latvians, but Latvian anarchists, eh?' The eyes were bright and shrewd. 'There are some. We have here in Melbourne the Nagiakas, the Zmowa Robotnicza, even the Red Cross—the Zenosis.'

'Who are they?'

'Miss Fisher, I don't think that I should tell you any more. These are dangerous people who will not bear investigation. They would not be pleased if they knew that you were even asking about them.'

'Why not? And did they ask my permission when they shot at me?'

'That must have been a mistake. They try not to draw attention to themselves.'

'Oh? Why?'

'Because they wish to finance the Revolution at home, of course. I'm sure that there are OGPU agents in Melbourne. And revenge against the relatives who are still in the homeland is not unknown. No, not unknown,' he mused, and a shadow of pain crossed his face, deepening the lines. Phryne had previously put his age at about thirty, but now thought that he must be ten years older.

'Am I putting you in danger by asking?'

'No, not I, Miss Fisher. But if you want me to tell you more it might be politic to move.'

'No, I disagree. The level of noise in this place is such that no one can overhear us. If we walk out together looking like conspirators then someone will certainly notice. Pray continue. Would you care for a cigarette?'

She offered her own case and he accepted.

Someone was attempting a medieval tune on an instrument which sounded like a trodden-on trumpet. Phryne asked one of the lovers what on earth it was.

'A crumhorn!' cried one of the young persons, disengaging his or her mouth from someone else's. 'It's authentic.'

'It certainly is,' yelled Phryne, and put a hand on Peter's arm. 'See? Lean a little closer and look like you are thinking of attempting to seduce a rich parvenue and no one will notice a thing.'

Phryne did not add that such things had been known to happen at Vera and Joseph Wilson's parties before; she had picked up a particularly beautiful lute-player once. And, now she came to think of it, a charming seaman who had unaccountably failed to make his ship the next morning and had to go out in the pilot boat.

Peter Smith put his arm around Phryne so that he could bring his mouth close enough to her ear.

'If you insist,' he sighed. 'So. There are three groups at least that could have provided your gunman.'

'Men. There were two of them.'

'Men,' he agreed. 'One has no name. The others are called the Latvian Revolutionary Alliance and the Free Latvia Party. I regret that they have been financing the Revolution by…you speak French?'

Phryne nodded. His arm was strong and he smelt delightfully of oranges. She was beginning to have designs upon him.

Peter Smith evidently felt the same, because he was holding her a lot closer than was tactically necessary. The crumhorn completed his piece and was replaced by three untuned recorders.

'I speak French.'

'*Illégalisme*,' he breathed in her ear. 'They have been robbing banks.'

'*Have* they?'

'With small success. They are not very efficient. But now the police are looking for all of them and they may have thought that you could know them again, and—'

'Decided to rub me out. Possibly.'

Phryne still had not mentioned the death of the young man and now felt that she could not.

'Why *illégalisme*? Why not get a job?'

'Ah, you do not understand. They are anarchists. Anarchists do not work. They refuse, they say, to exploit or be exploited. Therefore, the banks. In any case they could not earn sufficient for what they have in mind.'

'And what is that?'

Peter Smith paused. Phryne could see what he was thinking. A rich woman with no stake in the Revolution, how safe was her tongue? Would she be likely to tell anyone? Phryne stared into the dark-blue eyes with as limpid a gaze as she could possibly manage and saw the man make a decision.

'It is no secret, after all,' he said, softly. 'All of the Latvian community know of it. They want to train assassins in this law-abiding country of yours, Miss Fisher, and…'

'And?'

The cacophony produced by the recorders was jarring Phryne's ears. She leaned fully into the man's embrace and heard him whisper, '*Ils veulent assassiner Staline*—they want to kill Stalin.'

Chapter Four

'Absolutism tempered by assassination.'
Ernst Munster on the Russian Constitution

'Would you care to kiss me?' said Phryne. 'Just the hand. Then we shall go home to my house and you shall tell me more, if you will.'

Peter Smith kissed Phryne's hand lingeringly enough to convince any watcher that their alliance was not political and they clambered out of the party just as the recorders had been replaced by a very good flute.

'Phryne, just before you go.' Vera caught at her sleeve.

Phryne reached into her bag.

'What for this time, Vera?'

'The famine. In Africa.'

Phryne handed over two pounds. Vera gave her a receipt and said, 'Be careful of my Peter Smith, now, Phryne. I want him back. The World Revolution needs him.'

Phryne smiled a wicked smile and kissed Vera's cheek.

'You can have him back in time for the Revolution,' she whispered, and made a commendable exit without falling over too many bodies or the perambulator on the stair.

◇◇◇

'Home, Bert,' she ordered, climbing into the taxi and swallowing a few times to regain her hearing. Peter Smith did not speak on the journey, nor until he was being led into Phryne's parlour.

'This is your house?'

'Yes.'

'You are an aristocrat, then.'

'Not really. I spent all of my childhood on the verge of starvation and in dire poverty. Then the Great War killed a lot of young men and my father gained a title and I became a lady. Surprising, eh? What will you have?'

'A little whisky, I see that it is Laphroaig. A noble spirit. Hmm. So you know what it is to be poor?'

'Yes.'

Peter Smith relaxed a little and sat down in one of the comfortable chairs. He sipped the whisky and stared into the fire.

'They are not likely to succeed,' he commented. 'I agree.'

'I didn't say a thing!'

'No, but the thing is, on the face of it, absurd. To even get near to Stalin, a known Lett or a known anarchist, it would be impossible.'

'Oh, I don't know. There are always methods. No one can be guarded closely enough to resist a really determined assassin. Look at Tsar Alexander. He was surrounded with bodyguards and they still got him.'

'True. In any case I do not see the connection between a plot to kill Stalin and an attempt to kill you.'

'There is more to it,' said Phryne slowly. 'They were there to kill someone else. A young man. They had shot him.'

'He was dead?'

'Comprehensively.'

'And you saw them. So, that is reasonable. Naturally they would want to remove a witness. You relieve my mind. I would not like to think that my countrymen had taken leave of their senses.'

'Thank you so much. Do you approve of this…murder?'

'They must have had their reasons. He may have been a Bolshevik spy.'

'He can't have been. He was only a boy.'

'When I was such a boy, I and some others attacked Riga prison to free some of our brothers who were penned there. Some guards were killed. One of our men also.'

'And you escaped?'

'Yes. I had to flee the country. I left that night as supercargo in an English coaler.'

'Have you ever been back?'

'I? No,' he laughed painfully. 'There was nothing to take me back. My mother and my sister were shot by the secret police. I had no reason to go back. And I have reasons to stay here. *J'avais raison*. I have ties.'

Phryne was silent.

'However, that was a long time ago. I have been in many places since then.'

'These anarchists—the ones that are here—do you know them all?'

'Yes. Most of them.'

'And you don't know who the boy was, or why he was killed? I want to know,' Phryne said firmly. 'I don't care two hoots about Stalin. I am not interested in politics at all. But I want those two—I want them tried for murder and if he was a Bolshevik spy there must be better ways of dealing with them than to shoot them. Why not keep them and offer them false information? This is Australia and we cannot afford to have people exporting their revolutions here. If we have a revolution it must be an Australian one, or it can't possibly work.'

'You have reason,' he said stiffly, a literal translation of the French, Phryne realized. 'The police are doubtless in possession of all your information. Why not leave it to them?'

Phryne was tired and disinclined to argue. 'Perhaps that would be best. In any case, now that I have met you, Mr. Smith, perhaps we can improve our acquaintance. If you would like to call me in a few days, we can arrange something politically null. Dinner?'

'I shall certainly do myself the honour to call,' he said formally, accepted her card, and left. Phryne put herself wearily to bed and slept all night without dreams.

◇◇◇

Phryne breakfasted on croissants, strong *café au lait* and oranges. It was nine o'clock when she requested Mr. Butler to find the Anglican Sisterhood and put her in telephonic communication with the mother superior. It took twenty minutes, but eventually she was handed the phone and advised that Mother Theresa was willing to speak to her.

'Phryne Fisher here,' she said. 'Hello, Mother Theresa.'

An alto voice of some calm and humour replied, 'Mother Theresa here. What can I do for you, Miss Fisher?'

'I'm looking for a lost girl. Her name is Waddington-Forsythe. Do you have her, or have you seen her?'

'Why should I speak to you, Miss Fisher?'

'Because I feel that something very unpleasant may have happened to the child.'

'You are retained by Mr. Waddington-Forsythe?' asked the nun, with a nuance of distaste.

'Yes. I accepted the commission, thinking it was a prank or an unacceptable sweetheart, but I have met the family and now I have misgivings. Mother, have you seen her?'

The woman was silent.

Phryne said quickly, 'Have a heart, Mother Theresa! Don't make me comb all the brothels in Gertrude Street again.'

There was a shocked intake of breath. Mother Theresa asked sharply, 'Then this is not some adolescent tantrum? She is a godly and serious young woman, with a definite vocation. Have you any reason to think that…that such a fate may have befallen little Alicia?'

'No, but she is definitely missing. She isn't with any of her relatives, and her parents and her brother don't know where she is.'

'Her stepmother. Her own mother is dead, may she rest in peace.'

'You know the family?'

'Oh, yes. I beg your pardon for hesitating, Miss Fisher. Mr. Waddington-Forsythe is…'

'A pill. I know. Is Alicia with you?'

'No. Would it be of use to talk to me about the family? It might give you a clue.'

'Yes. When shall I come to see you?'

'Today, if you like. I am always at home, Miss Fisher.'

'I'll come directly,' promised Phryne, was blessed, and rang off. Phryne went to get dressed in suitable convent-visiting clothes, wondering which Theresa she had taken as her saint. Theresa of Avila, Phryne guessed, a strong-minded Spaniard who had bishops hiding under their desks, rather than the sentimental and girlish Therese of the Flowers, from Liseux.

'Dot, take a coat, we are going to visit a convent. What shall I wear?'

'Something lavish, Miss.'

'Lavish?'

'Yes, Miss, it will please the little girls to see a lady in nice clothes. It always did when I was at school. The sapphire blue suit, Miss, with the silk coat and a nice hat.'

'It's not a Catholic convent, Dot, it's an Anglican one.'

'I didn't know they had convents. But it will be the same, Miss.'

'Sapphire and silk it shall be, and that darling blue hat with the anemones. That should be lavish enough. Are you coming?'

'If you want me, Miss.'

'Of course I do.'

Dot smiled, provided undergarments and the suit, then sprinkled Phryne with attar of roses.

'Why roses?'

'It's the only scent the nuns don't object to, because of the miracle of St. Elizabeth of Bohemia,' explained Dot patiently. 'And there are no scents in convents but honest soap and baking bread. When a lady visited we used to stand around her, sniffing.'

Phryne insisted that Dot have some attar too, so that they would match. Dot took her azure coat and donned her embroidered afternoon tea dress, pulling on a sensible hat and driving gloves.

'Where is this convent, Miss?'

'Eltham. Mr. Butler is driving. We shall sit in the back and be ladies, for a change. We might have to stay overnight, so bring a nightie and pack one for me. I'll be downstairs arranging for a picnic basket.'

Phryne negotiated with Mrs. Butler for a luncheon basket and the loan of her husband for the day. Mr. Butler joyfully dusted off his chauffeur's cap and got out the maps. It was not often that Phryne allowed anyone to drive her prized car.

Such was Phryne's strength of character and the efficiency of her household, that she and Dot were seated in a car loaded with travelling rugs, hats, overnight bags and picnic baskets by ten o'clock, and Mr. Butler was steering the great car out into The Esplanade on the way to Eltham. Phryne disliked being driven in her own car, but she had an effect to make and Dot to amuse. Dot disliked cars under any circumstances and was only reconciled to the Hispano-Suiza because of a recently discovered aversion to trains.

'Tell me about St. Elizabeth of Bohemia, Dot.'

'She was the wife of a nasty prince,' said Dot. 'We are going to hit that truck!'

'No we aren't. Go on. If you keep interrupting, I shall never get the story straight, and think of the peril to my immortal soul.' Sobered by this reflection, Dot pulled herself together.

'As I say, a nasty cruel prince who would not let her give food to the poor. So she used to smuggle it out in her basket. He had threatened to have her killed if he caught her giving any of his bread to the beggars. One day he grabbed her when she was carrying a basket full of food and demanded to know what she had in it. She said, 'Roses,' and he didn't believe it and tore the basket open. It was full of roses. God had saved her so that she could keep feeding the poor.'

'Gosh, Dot, what a story! And she must have got such a shock when he opened the basket. Imagine, there she is, expecting to be killed on the spot, possibly even rather liking the prospect of going to Heaven and leaving this cruel man, and then saved, suddenly, miraculously. It must have been like a blow in the face.'

'I suppose it would have been,' agreed Dot, dragging her eyes away from the Plenty Road milestones which seemed to be fleeting past with indecent speed. 'Where are we now, Miss?'

'Preston. Cheer up. We'll be out of the suburbs soon and there will be less traffic. I spoke to your young constable this morning. He's rather nice, Dot. Do you like him?'

Dot stared at Phryne, reddening.

'Yes, Miss, I like him well enough.'

'He's about to ask you to help him in a spot of detection. I suggested that he go to the Latvian Club and sit in on one of their meetings, with a young lady as cover, and he thought of you. He's a Catholic, by the way,' added Phryne.

'Oh, Miss,' wailed Dot. 'What shall I do?'

'It won't do any harm if he just asks, Dot. You can always say no.'

'But I don't want to say no,' confessed Dot. Phryne chuckled.

'Then say yes, Dot. What could be more proper than a meeting of the Latvian Club? I'm sure that it will be all right. He just wants to observe, you know. Have you got the thermos? I could do with some tea,' said Phryne, to distract Dot.

She poured the tea, already sugared, and they sipped in silence. Mr. Butler was a very good driver, and the roads were almost empty. Farmland stretched out on either side, with a few scattered houses. Reservoir was approaching. Phryne lit a gasper and enjoyed the scenery. The very first plum blossoms of spring were decorating the landscape. 'Rough winds do shake the darling buds of May,' she murmured. 'And summer's lease hath all too short a date.'

Eltham was beautiful, and the Convent of the Holy Spirit was awesome. Phryne reflected how proud the gold-rich ex-digger who had built it must have been of his beautiful house. His wife, she was told by a chatty guidebook, had been born in

Paris, and had taken Directoire ideas and married them to Old British Empire with verandahs. It was built of red brick with cornices and gargoyles and was so very, very vulgar that it was magnificent. Its total disregard of all canons of taste was dramatic and oddly endearing.

'My Sacred Lord,' exclaimed Dot, startled, and crossed herself.

'Yes, it is rather…er…actually I can't think of a word that adequately describes it. According to the guidebook, the sisterhood acquired it after the original owner drank himself to death celebrating the end of the Boer War. They've been here ever since. I wonder which of the three doors I can see is the front one? And those gargoyles seem familiar…aha, I have it. Notre Dame, of course.'

A very tidy bevy of small girls approached at a convent-trained walk, stopped in front of the visitors and stared up at them. The Anglicans appeared to detest the flesh as much as the Catholics, to judge from the ugliness of the school uniforms. The girls were clad in dark serge, box-pleated and ankle-length, white shirts in a painful condition of starch and the most pot-shaped hats Phryne had ever seen. They smelt of good honest soap and scrubbing, and their hair was strained painfully back from rosy faces.

'Miss Fisher?' asked the tallest girl. 'Mother sent us to escort you.'

The girls were feeding their eyes on Phryne's clothes, and on Dot's. Dot had been right about the scent. Phryne, surrounded by small mushroom buttons which bobbed about her, could distinctly hear them sniffing.

The left-hand of the three doors was the front door, panelled in blue glass like the wings of tropical butterflies, and they were conducted down a corridor which had been polished glassy. The walls and ceiling were stencilled in burnt orange, umber, mustard and wine-red with dancing maidens and pagan gods. Phryne wondered that the convent management had not papered over them.

The convoy anchored before a wooden door which appeared to have been made out of a solid block of mahogany. The tallest girl tapped and retreated, then the door swung open and the children vanished.

Phryne turned to thank them but they were gone. She raised an eyebrow and Dot nodded. She too had learned to vanish with silent celerity when a similar door had swung open in her own convent.

A nun who appeared to have vinegar running in her veins paused in order to disapprove properly of the Reverend Mother's visitors, then ushered them across the shining sea of parquet to another door, which she flung open with a shattering crash before announcing: 'Your callers, Reverend Mother!'

The woman sitting at the desk stood up, winced a little at the noise, and smiled.

Phryne went forward to take the Mother's hand, and was invited to sit down in a chair of penitential straitness.

'I am Phryne Fisher, and this is my confidential secretary Miss Williams. I hope that I have not interrupted you.'

'No, no, not at all. I am seriously concerned by the fears you expressed for little Alicia. Not a very stable girl, I admit, but with a background like that...'

'What was her background?'

Dark brown eyes, hard to read. The hands, long and fine, laid one in another like an opera singer's. The face a smooth oval, unlined, serene, but a soft full mouth, tucked firmly in at the corners as though her sense of the ridiculous had survived years of relentless theology. Charming.

'Her mother died when she was seven—a painful, long, drawn-out death. Cancer. The Lord give her rest. Then her father, who should have been old enough to know better, married a woman forty years younger than he was, although I believe that there was nothing *known* against her character. Alicia is a strong minded and chaste young woman. I believe that she found her father's behaviour disgusting. Who could blame her? The situation was made worse by the way her brother reacted to the new bride. Both her father and her brother were besotted with the woman and there was no love left over for Alicia, do you see? Not a pleasant situation for Alicia.'

Phryne nodded. She saw.

'Her father refused to leave her here with us, and took her away to a secular school in the city when she expressed a vocation. All I could do was to tell her that a true vocation could not be denied and the Lord would find a way. I have almost been expecting her. But she is not here and she has not been here. I will call her two closest friends, if you would like, who can confirm this.'

Phryne nodded again. Dot appeared to be bearing up fairly well against an onslaught of remembered awe.

'Sister Constantine?' The Reverend Mother addressed her acidic secretary. 'Could you find the Bevan sisters and bring them to me? Tell them that they are not in any trouble. I merely want to talk to them.'

The sister vanished in a flounce of habit, slamming the door again.

'I fear that Sister Constantine is of the old school,' she apologized. 'She does not believe in softness and courtesy. Since she has been with us she really has improved.'

Phryne wondered what Sister Constantine had been in private life. A bricklayer, she decided, or one of Whelan the Wrecker's prize operatives.

Two girls were shoved into the room and stood transfixed before the desk, tongue tied.

'This is the Honourable Phryne Fisher, and Miss Williams, girls. This is Nicola Bevan and this is her sister Anne. Now, girls, we need to know when you last saw Alicia Waddington-Forsythe. Speak up, now. You aren't in any trouble. We just want to know.'

Nicola burst into tears. Dot took charge.

'Come here,' she invited, opening her purse. When the girls came close enough she popped a bullseye into each mouth.

'Now you tell the lady what she wants to know,' she encouraged. 'Reverend Mother isn't angry with you.'

Anne Bevan tucked the bullseye joyfully into her check and smiled.

'I have told these ladies that the last time we saw Alicia was three weeks ago,' began the Mother, leading the witness in a most undesirable fashion. Nicola took courage from the bullseye and the proximity of the sapphire suit and blurted out, 'Oh, no, Reverend Mother, we saw her on Wednesday.'

'Wednesday of this week?' asked Phryne quickly. Nicola nodded.

'Where?'

'Why, here, Miss, at the school, she had a bag with her and said that she had run away and she was going to see Reverend Mother and get her postulancy…'

'She never saw me!' exclaimed the Mother. 'Are you sure, Nicola?' Nicola nodded vigorously.

'What time did you see her?' asked Phryne.

'Late, Miss, it was after dinner. She said that she came on the late train. She called us down into the courtyard and she had her bag and everything and I expected her to be at breakfast but she wasn't and what's happened to her? Is she lost?'

'Yes. I believe that she is. But that is a secret, both of you. Do you hear me? Not one word to anyone else, or I shall be severely displeased.' Reverend Mother had authority. 'Have you any more questions, Miss Fisher?'

'What was she wearing?'

'Blue uniform and white blouse, Miss.'

'Did she have her diary with her?'

'Oh, I expect so, Miss. She always carried it. And she said she was going straight to see you, Reverend Mother.'

'All right, girls. You may spend the rest of this period in the Chapel praying for your friend, for God will protect her wherever she is. Off you go, now.'

Dot handed over another bullseye each and the Bevan sisters withdrew on tiptoes, incandescent with their secret.

'Sister Constantine!' called Mother Theresa, in a tone of steely command. The nun edged reluctantly into the room.

'You kept her away from me, did you not, Sister?'

'I don't know what you mean, Mother.'

'Yes, you do, Sister. That miserable Alicia Waddington-Forsythe ran away from home and came here for postulancy and refuge, and you sent her away, did you not? God knows the secrets of all hearts, and while I do not claim Divinity I have my share of sense. Tell me what happened.'

'She came marching in as though she owned the place, and complaining of her stepmother. I did not want you to be disturbed by such talk, so I told her that she no longer had any connection with the school and she could not be a nun here and that she should go back to her father.'

'You sent her out, fourteen years old, despairing, and alone?' Mother Theresa's voice was as cold as the grave, into which she evidently hoped that Sister Constantine would sink. The secretary nodded.

'You are suspended from all duties, Sister, and will remain henceforward in your cell on bread and water. There you will meditate on what our Saviour said about charity. You will stay there until the priest comes, to whom I recommend that you make a full confession. Go now. You have fallen into mortal sin, Sister Constantine.' The woman turned away. Phryne seized her sleeve.

'Wait. Where did she go?'

'I didn't notice,' muttered the sour voice. 'Away. Toward the station. And good riddance! Holier-than-thou little madam, with her beautiful house and her beautiful brother and her money.'

Sister Constantine left, slamming the door with a deafening crash.

'Well, that's torn it,' commented Phryne. The Reverend Mother snatched up a particularly revolting statuette of the infant Samuel and threw it to shatter against the stencilled nymphs on her wall.

Chapter Five

'Les enfants terrible' (The embarrassing young)
Paul Gavarni

'So, what did the Reverend Mother do then?' asked Ruth Fisher, née Collins.

'She recovered her serenity—by a huge effort—and asked us to tea, but Dot and I were fairly unnerved by then, so we piled back into the car and Mr. Butler drove us home. On the way we stopped at all the likely places and asked if anyone had seen Alicia. We had several sightings of her before she came to the school, and none after, but it was dark by then.'

'Ooh, it sounds spooky,' commented Ruth, taking another piece of fruit cake as a prophylactic against further shocks. 'What do you think, Jane?'

Jane Fisher, née Graham, stared gravely out the window of the cake shop and shook her head.

'I don't know, Ruthie, it sounds bad, doesn't it? What if she never left the convent? Maybe they've buried her in the cellar, like in…' she blushed and bit into her apricot tart. Phryne laughed.

'What have you been reading, girls? *The Awful Adventures of Maria Monk*?'

From the shocked glances it was clear that this was the source of their ideas.

'Finish those cakes and we'll take a little walk. Let's decide which cake we shall take home for Dot and the Butlers. What shall it be? Mrs. Rosenbaum makes a lovely fruit cake.'

'Brandy snaps? No, Mrs. B. makes them herself. Chocolate cake,' said Jane. 'The one with jam and cream.'

'Good choice,' agreed Ruth, and Phryne paid for the tea and ordered a chocolate cake to be sent to her house before they emerged onto the street into pale spring sunshine.

Ruth and Jane were the human results of Phryne's investigation into a mystery a month before. Phryne had adopted Jane as the only way of keeping her safe. Ruth had been Jane's best friend and fellow-captive, so Phryne had adopted her too, feeling that Jane would need some company in Phryne's rackety house. They were both at the Presbyterian Ladies' College and doing well. Jane was university material and wanted to be a doctor.

For the moment, however, they were both concentrating on the disappearance of their school fellow. The brown plaits and the black plaits met as Ruth whispered to Jane, and Jane nodded.

'We think that we ought to tell you about Alicia,' announced Jane abruptly. 'Even though it is sneaking. After all, she might be in real trouble, mightn't she?'

Phryne assented, leading the way across St. Kilda Road onto the foreshore, where a number of bathers were braving the weather.

'Tell me,' she invited. 'You can rely on my confidence.'

Ruth took Jane's hand. Phryne surveyed them, pleased at the progress which had been made since they had been rescued, starved and slatternly, from a dreadful boarding house in Seddon. Jane had grown at least an inch and both of them had put on weight. Their eyes were clear and their skin rosy under the influence of safety and chocolate cake. Possibly as a result of early privation, Ruth had announced an intention to become a cook, which had endeared her to Mrs. Butler. The expenditure of a certain sum had clothed them suitably and fashionably in yellow and red, and they made a bright and cheering sight in the watery sun, which was just making up its mind to shine.

'You were saying, Ruth,' prompted Phryne. 'Did you both know Alicia?'

'Yes, Miss Phryne, she was in the same form as us. She did Latin and mathematics with Jane and English with me. She was a worm.'

'What do you mean, a worm?'

'She liked secrets, you see. She wormed them out of people and then she got what she wanted from them because she knew the secret,' explained Jane. 'She tried it on us, we aren't just telling you gossip.'

'What was your secret?'

'Why, that we were domestic servants in a boarding house, and that you adopted us.' Jane was patient. 'She found out about it and then tried to blackmail us into...into...'

'Come along, Ruthie, Jane, tell me your sins.' Phryne was serious.

'There's a club of us, Miss Phryne, the ones who don't come from the same backgrounds as the other girls. We have great times. We put all our money together to buy Fleischer cakes and eat them in the big oak tree. You know.'

Phryne nodded. She knew.

'Well, Alicia wanted to join, and we said that she couldn't, because she didn't qualify and anyway...'

'She is a worm,' agreed Phryne. 'Yes, and...?'

'So she said she'd tell everyone about where we came from, and Ruthie and me, we told her to tell everyone, we didn't care. We are very lucky,' said Jane, glancing admiringly up at Phryne in her shady straw and grass-green dress. 'We know that. So...'

'So, she went off muttering. "Exit, pursued by a bear,"' quoted Ruth, who was studying *The Winter's Tale*. 'And we didn't hear any more about her. But she had a diary, and she wrote all these secrets in it. A purple leather book, bound, with *Firenze* on the front. What's *Firenze*, Miss Phryne?'

'It's a place where they make good leather—in Italy. We call it Florence. An expensive diary. Did she always carry it with her?'

'Yes, always. Beastly girl,' said Jane, with sudden loathing. 'She caused a lot of trouble, you know. What about poor Miss Ellis?'

'What about her? Who is Miss Ellis?'

'She was a music teacher. She used to drink. Alicia spied on her until she caught her with a bottle and then told the Head, and got Miss Ellis sacked.'

'She sounds like a detestable young woman.'

'Yes. But Mary Tachell would know more about her. She is her best friend.'

'We shall invite Mary to tea,' decided Phryne. 'What's she like?'

'Pale and peepy and weak,' said Jane dismissively. 'Do we have to?'

'For my investigation, yes.'

'All right. I'll ring her up when we get home,' agreed Ruth. For Phryne, she would entertain a dozen Marys.

◇◇◇

They returned to the house, where Mr. Butler was just replacing the telephone.

'Ah, Miss Fisher, a Mr. Peter Smith has called. He said that if there is no objection, he will visit tonight at about nine. He says that he has some information for you.'

'Good. I'm going up for a nap, Mr. B. Could you get a telephone number for Miss Ruth? Oh, Jane, Ember has missed you!'

Jane buried her face into the midnight-black fur of a cat which had wreathed himself around her neck and was purring like an engine.

Pleased with the excellent condition of her strays, Phryne mounted the stairs to fling off her hat and lie down with the latest detective story which the bookshop had sent her.

◇◇◇

Mary Tachell arrived, chauffeured in a huge black Bentley, two hours later, in time for a four o'clock tea of startling proportions. The centrepiece of the loaded table was the bought cake, and Mrs. Butler had laid out sandwiches, jelly, cream cakes, scones, and plain cakes. Phryne presided over the table and the girls introduced Mary.

She was an undersized creature, with pale blue eyes swimming behind thick lenses and a mass of white-blonde hair which was supposed to be restrained by an Alice band but which was perpetually escaping. She ate as though she had been through a long winter's famine. Phryne did not try to question Mary. Instead she left the strategy to her adoptive daughters, who were showing a fine natural talent for intrigue.

'Have you seen Alicia lately?' asked Ruth. 'Have some more jelly.'

'No.' The reply was muffled. 'She's run away.'

'Run away! Where to?'

'The sisterhood,' announced Mary. This was the most exciting thing which had happened to her in years and she was not going to waste any of her sensation. 'A convent. In Eltham.'

'When? Look out, your hair's in the cream.'

Ruth extracted the strand with a deft twitch. Unlike Jane, who could fall over a piece of string, Ruth was forceful and neat in her actions.

'She ran away on Wednesday. She said that she couldn't stand the secret any more.'

'What secret?'

Mary confined her answer to looking wise and stuffing a cream cake into her mouth.

'Don't be silly, Jane, there's no secret,' scorned Ruth, and Mary rose to the bait like a trout.

'There is so! Alicia said so!'

'What was it, then, this secret?' Ruth's voice was dismissive.

'She wouldn't tell me, but it was something to do with her family. She said that she couldn't stay in her father's house any more once she knew about it and she was running away to be a nun.'

And what an impediment to that peaceful community she would have been, thought Phryne, taking a brandy snap. Fortunate for the nuns that she had not stayed. Alicia could have wreaked ruin on them. But perhaps she had been happy there and would have been a good and devout sister.

'Have you heard from her since she went?' Just the question which Phryne was burning to ask. She cast an appreciative glance upon Jane.

'No. But she hasn't got her diary.'

'How do you know?'

'Not telling. Why are you so interested, anyway? You wouldn't let us join your club.'

'We asked you to tea,' said Ruth. 'You can at least talk to us.'

'Won't. I'm going home. Why are you asking about Alicia?'

Both girls looked at Phryne for instructions. She said easily, 'Alicia isn't at the sisterhood.'

'She isn't?'

'No. I've been there. She went to Eltham, but she did not stay. She has been missing since Wednesday. She might be in trouble. You can help me find her.'

'Oh, Miss Fisher!' cried Mary. 'She didn't tell me she was going anywhere else. She said she was going to be a nun.'

'She went to the sisterhood, but she met a nasty woman there who sent her away. Now, where else could she have gone?'

Phryne could see the sordid row of houses in Gertrude Street which she might have to search. She sighed. Mary Tachell had begun to cry, and was being patted by Jane. Ruth was thinking, her eyes as bright as pins.

'Maybe she's been kidnapped,' she commented.

'Who'd want her?' asked Phryne, rhetorically.

Mary wailed, 'She was my friend! I liked her, even if no one else did, and she was good to me when I was lonely and no one would talk to me. What can have happened to her? She said she was going to be…'

'…a nun. I know. Now think, if you are fond of her. Where else could she have gone?'

'I don't know, Miss Fisher. I really don't know. But she was going to send for her diary.'

'Aha. That diary. Where is it?'

'Not telling.'

'All right, but tell me this, is it in a safe place? Where no one is likely to find it?'

Mary nodded. Phryne waved a cautioning hand at the girls.

'All right. That's enough for one day. Have another scone. Mrs. Butler makes good scones. You think about it, and when you decide to give the diary to me so that I might be able to find Alicia, then you call me. Perhaps I should contact your parents,' mused Phryne. 'I really should not be asking you questions without them knowing.'

Mary shied like a frightened horse. The whites of her eyes showed.

'No, no, please don't tell them! It's in a hollow tree in Domain Gardens. We used to walk there. I'll show you.'

'Wise decision, Mary. Tomorrow we shall call on you and you can give me the diary and then, if we find Alicia, I will give it back to her and explain why you gave it to me. It will be all right. Alicia will understand. Now have some more tea and wipe your face. You have done your best to find your friend and now I will do my best. It's all right, Mary!'

Mary was a biddable creature. She wiped her face with her napkin and took another cup of tea and was comforted. Phryne left the girls to finish their tea and went to take a bath, disgusted with the success of her methods.

Ruth and Jane, on the other hand, were delighted.

'You did that very well, Miss Phryne,' said Jane as Phryne descended the great stair clad in an afternoon dress of handkerchief-pointed crepe. 'She didn't have a chance to lie.'

'She was easy. It was a shame to take her money, and such methods must not be used except for a good purpose, so don't congratulate me, girls, and for God's sake don't emulate me unless you really need to know something. What would you like to do now?'

'Try on our new dresses,' said Ruth.

Phryne sat in her cool parlour and watched them as they emerged from their room, clad in several changes of new clothes, culminating in one evening dress each. Madam Partlett had designed them, and each was 'Correct, Miss Fisher, and *à la jeune fille*.' Jane's dress was heliotrope, to emphasise her chestnut hair, and Ruth's was of pale cyclamen to set off her dark skin, brown eyes, and black hair. There were matching shoes and one short string each of small pearls.

'When I am taller I shall wear wine colours., announced Ruth, smoothing down her straight front. 'Wine and amber.'

'I shall always like this colour,' Jane was looking at herself in the big glass with astonishment. 'It makes me look quite different. But when shall we wear them?'

'We shall go to the ballet on Tuesday night, as long as no other developments happen. Even if they do, Dr. MacMillan will take you. It is the Russian Ballet and they are doing *Petroushka*, which you will love. I would like to see it again but I might not be able to. It depends. Now, tonight I am entertaining Mr. Smith, who may have some important information for me, so I shall go up directly after dinner.'

'Is he staying?' asked Jane, trying to get a back view.

'Don't know.'

'Well, I've got all that homework, anyway. Eh, Ruth?'

'Geography,' groaned Ruth. 'Perhaps I shall have a shawl, a long traily one.'

She snatched up Phryne's shawl and glided around the room, watching the effect of the following fringes. Phryne reflected that in a few years' time Ruth would be a force to be reckoned with. Jane, on the other hand, was not really interested in clothes. She was born plain and she did not seem to mind.

'And Latin, and English, we've got to finish *The Winter's Tale*.'

'Well, it's a good play. You should enjoy it.'

'Mmm, yes, but you'd think that they would have taught him to spell. How now, varlet,' said Jane. 'Give Miss Phryne's shawl back and let's go and read it.'

Ruth hung the shawl carefully over the back of a chair and followed Jane into their room to continue her attack on England's Greatest Poet with some signs of enthusiasm.

◇◇◇

The girls, whose appetite was prodigious, dined with Phryne at six o'clock on *Soupe Provençale*, veal cutlets and fruit. Phryne was eagerly anticipating the advent of apricots and nectarines and her special favourite, white peaches, which spring was promising. Ruth and Jane took their baths as ordered and retired to their room, where Phryne could hear the buzz of Shakespearean dialogue with occasional breaks while they puzzled out what he meant.

'But why is he jealous of her? She hasn't done anything!' protested Ruth. Jane murmured some reply and Phryne took herself upstairs to resume study of her shocker until Peter Smith should arrive.

Chapter Six

*'Tout passe, tout casse, tout lasse' (Everything
passes, everything breaks, everything palls)*
French proverb

Phryne flung the detective story against the wall. She had guessed
the murderer in the third chapter and was not patient. She struck
the author's name from her list of books to be ordered just as
she heard 'Mr. Peter Smith' announced. Dot brought him up to
the salon, where he asked for whisky and water and sank into
one of the plush chairs.

Phryne dismissed Dot with a nod, but her maid drew her
to the door.

'Constable Collins has called, Miss. I'm going to the Latvian
Club with him on Wednesday night.'

'Good. I'm taking the girls to the ballet on Tuesday, so I'll be
home if you need me. Not that you are likely to…'

Dot smiled. She was sure that she could handle Hugh Collins,
but Latvians, being foreign and possibly dangerous, were another
matter.

Dot closed the door and Phryne poured a stiff whisky for her
guest.

'There is something going on,' announced Peter Smith. 'And I do not like it, because I cannot find out what it is.'

His English was perfect, the accent blameless, but when excited his diction was too precise. He gulped down the drink and held out his glass for another. Phryne gave him unlabelled. There was no point in wasting Laphroaig on a distracted man.

'What is going on? You mean the plot to kill Stalin?'

'No, no, I already knew about that. You have stumbled on something nasty, Miss Fisher.'

'Call me Phryne, please. And I can hardly be said to have been anything but an innocent bystander. They did not know that I was coming, did they? I did not know myself. Have some more whisky and take off your coat. It is better to be comfortable if you are worried.'

Peter Smith cast Phryne an appreciative smile, took off his coat revealing a collarless white shirt, and sipped at the second whisky.

He had dark-blue eyes and hollows under them that spoke of past privation. As he rolled up his sleeves she noticed several long-healed scars ringing his wrists. He smiled.

'When they caught me, the Russians, they put me in shackles, because they thought that I was a dangerous revolutionary. Which, of course, I was,' he added complacently. 'And they did not take them off for three months. I was fixed to a wall and I slumped into the chains when I slept; thus I was galled.'

'When was that?'

'A long time ago.' He sipped his drink. 'And in another country. My past does not matter in this clean land, which has no heavy burden of history to deform the backs of its children. That is why I came here.'

'When did you come here?'

'In the year 10 or so, I believe. I have worked on the wharf since then, which is a good place to work, being well paid and independent. I do not wish to be any man's serf.'

'One thing you can say about wharfies, they are not serfs,' agreed Phryne. 'I have friends working there.'

'Have you, indeed? Strange friends for a lady.'

'I'm getting sick of this!' exclaimed Phryne. 'Listen, I was not born to the purple, you know. I lived in the streets and starved when I had to, and this aristocratic layer is mere overlay on an impeccable working-class base. Get that clear, if you please. I am rich, and I enjoy money but, like Queen Elizabeth, cast me out into any part of my realm in my petticoat and I would be what I am. Do I make myself clear?'

She was expecting him to be affronted. She was not expecting him to put down his glass, drop to one knee, and kiss her hand with great respect.

'Pardon, madam, pardon. I have been guilty of *classisme*. You are a unique phenomenon, Phryne. I have never met anyone like you before, and I have met princesses in my time.'

'So have I.' Phryne remembered the Princesse de Grasse and chuckled. She occasionally regretted the loss of the princesse, who had gone back to Paris, taking her grandson the beautiful Sasha with her, leaving Phryne without a lover for at least ten minutes. Phryne restored Peter Smith to his chair and asked if he had eaten.

It appeared he had not. Phryne telephoned to Mrs. Butler for sandwiches and the leftovers from the girls' high tea. A tray was delivered by Mr. Butler. Peter Smith ate as though he was famished.

Poor, Phryne thought, though that might be from political conviction rather than lack of coin. He was not precisely thin, few wharfies were thin, because of the muscle they built up by carrying hundred-weights of wheat in an eight-hour shift, also the beer which they consumed in great quantities to dilute the dust. Peter Smith absorbed four sandwiches, eight little cakes and the remaining slice of chocolate cake, washed down with another whisky, then sat back and sighed. Some of the tension was gone from his face.

He really was very good looking. High cheekbones, slightly slanted eyes with dark lashes, and finely drawn mouth and chin. His hair was cut brutally short, dark brown streaked with grey.

'There. Isn't that better? Being frightened is one thing; being hungry and frightened is another.'

'Madam, all my life I seem to have been hungry and frightened.' He settled deeper into the plush chair and stretched his legs. Phryne said nothing, and without cue, Peter Smith began to talk.

'That is what is good about Australia. There is so little history. Regrettably we refuge-seekers have brought it with us. All our pain, all our grudges, all our atrocities. One does not forget murder, assassination, the death of children. It is impossible. And then, we clump together. It is sweet to hear your own language, your own idioms; to recall the old country. With this, however, comes the old feuds. It is ridiculous to continue our emnities here, but we continue them. Just today I spoke to three people, on whom the claws of the old battles are still fixed. It makes me very sad to think of them. Poor men. They have no chance of succeeding; and they are cowards, also. They should fight their battle in Latvia, not here. What use can a bank robbery here have for the fall of Stalin? How long can such a man as Stalin last, anyway? So, I spoke to all of them, attempting to ascertain the name and allegiance of the young man who was killed in madam's presence. I do not know his name, but a woman will go and identify him tomorrow, at Russell Street, and if madam were to befriend her…'

'Madam takes your point.'

'Good.'

'However, there is something else.' Phryne sat down on the hearthrug at Peter's feet, looking up at the strained face.

'Yes,' admitted the man. 'There is something else. I will tell you, Phryne. I trust you.'

'So you may.'

Peter Smith looked down into Phryne's countenance, then up into the pink mirror which showed him his own face wreathed in green ceramic vine leaves. Even in the salons of the *Grandes Horizontales* in Paris where he had once been as a young and disapproving revolutionary, he did not recall such pervasive eroticism. The demi-mondaine had been stupid, with intellectual pretensions. Sitting at his feet was a very intelligent woman.

He sighed, closed his eyes, and continued, 'A bank robbery is planned for the near future. This week, I believe. The group which is carrying it out is armed. They have, among other things, a Lewis gun.'

'A *Lewis gun*! A machine-gun? Are you sure?'

Phryne had heard Lewis guns in the Great War. It was a portable machine-gun with drum magazine and its power over a line of innocent civilians did not bear thinking of. Phryne sat up and put an urgent hand on Peter Smith's knee.

'I am sure. I have seen it. They showed it to me. They were proud of it. Fools! Did they not learn anything in London? The Houndsditch massacre, the Tottenham outrage, the Siege of Sidney Street? They were burned to death in that house…'

He stopped suddenly. The moment poised on a knife's edge. Phryne held her breath, biting back the question, 'Were you in the siege?' One wrong word and Peter Smith would shut up like a clam. He stared into the mirror. When he spoke again it was in a calm voice.

'They have learned nothing. Anarchists are devoted to nothingness. Do not misunderstand me. I still hope for the Revolution. I have given to it my mother and my sister and the young woman whom I was to marry, and my village was bombed flat by the big guns. But outrages in Melbourne will bring political repression, and we will lose those freedoms which make Australia dear to me. And they will not listen. I am no longer at the forefront.' He took Phryne's hand in his. 'I cannot control the strong passions of the young.'

'And you cannot tell me any more?' asked Phryne gently, expecting his reply.

'I cannot tell you any more. But if you find Maria Aliyena, she will be susceptible to your charm. The dead young man, I am told, was her cousin, and she was very fond of him.'

'Why did they kill him?'

'He got drunk in the Watersider Hotel and told the whole bar that he was a bank robber and had a machine-gun.'

'And they killed him for that?'

'They killed him for that.'

Peter Smith sagged down into Phryne's arms. It was not until she felt tears on her neck that she realized he was weeping. His back was knotted, his hands clutched her, and when his lips found her mouth he kissed her as though he was clinging to a plank in a shipwreck.

Surprised, but pleased, Phryne hitched a hip forward so that she was lying at full length on the sheepskin hearthrug and responded to bottomless kisses, his mouth hot and wet and demanding.

They lay together for almost an hour. Phryne was delighted by the kisses and the emotional depth which he exhibited, but she had no mind to take advantage of Slavic sorrow. She pulled away, out of the strong arms and the clutch of the calloused hands.

'What is wrong?'

'I want to give you a chance to decide if you want to get up and go home,' said Phryne collectedly. Peter Smith stared at her for a good minute in astonishment, then began to laugh.

'Oh, Phryne, as I said, you are unique. Do you not desire me?'

'Of course.'

His eyes filled with tears again, spilling down over the cheekbones and into his smile. 'I want you,' he whispered. 'Comfort me against age and the prospect of all I have fought for being wasted by fools. You are the most wonderful woman I have ever met.'

Phryne knelt, shedding her crêpe dress, and unbuttoned his workman's shirt revealing his strong throat, burnt brown by the sun, and a small round tattoo on his collarbone: a capital A in a circle, done in blue ink.

She bent and kissed the tattoo, removing the shirt. His hands found the fastenings of her chemise and the garters rolled down her thighs as though they had a life of their own.

Peter Smith, stripped, was strong and muscular. He had a star-shaped bullet scar on his chest, which Phryne kissed gently when they lay together in her big bed on the green sheets.

'It missed my heart,' he murmured. 'But you have not. What can I give you, Phryne, for the gift of your body?'

'The gift of yours,' said Phryne, trapping his mouth again. Sweet, sweet, she thought, the touch of these practised hands, the skin almost scratching as they swept across her belly. She moaned and turned into his arms, caressing the scarred back. His face reared above her, a Slavic mask, the mouth reddened and swollen from kisses, the blue eyes burning.

Consummation was so close and sweet that she cried aloud.

◇◇◇

Phryne woke eight hours later when Dot tapped at the door. It appeared to be Monday, and morning. Phryne asked for coffee and croissants for two, and padded back to the big bed and drew the curtains. The man woke, sat up straight, and then relaxed back into the embrace of the pillows.

'Oh, Phryne,' he murmured. 'I thought that I was back in prison, and that I had dreamed you. You are the sort of dream which comes to a man in prison. The essence of all sensuality. Come here and let me hold you close, or I shall not be convinced that you are not a vision.'

Phryne subsided back into his arms, sated and sleepy and pleased that he was not going to recoil in that inexplicable way that some men did.

Mr. Butler put the breakfast tray on the table in the salon.

'Let go, Peter, I need coffee. Come and have some breakfast.'

Peter released her with unflattering celerity. This man was definitely underfed. He ate most of the fresh rolls and a lot of jam and butter. Phryne nibbled at one croissant and drank most of the coffee. She never felt very well early in the morning.

'I must get dressed, Peter, if I am to catch Maria Aliyena at Russell Street.'

'This is true, although sad,' he agreed. 'I may return?'

'You may. Tell me. Do the anarchist women have that tattoo, as well?'

'Yes. On the left breast. There,' he demonstrated.

'Lend me your shoulder, then, just for a moment.'

Peter Smith sat uncomplainingly as Phryne took a piece of thin paper and traced the tattoo with a pencil.

'You are not going to be tattooed?' he asked in horror, pausing with a piece of croissant half-way to his mouth.

'No, but I might do something with indelible pencil.'

'That will not do. These marks are always in blue ink.'

'I'll think of something,' said Phryne. 'Now, you can have the bathroom, while I find something to wear. What does one wear to identify a body and snare a grieving woman?'

She did not expect an answer but he called from the bathroom, 'A black dress, well-worn, with soup down the front.'

Phryne laughed and rummaged in her wardrobe, finding a black dress which had seen better days, and was wobbly about the hem due to being badly laundered. She had kept it because she was minded to demand her money back. She farewelled Peter at her door after he had splashed vigorously and found his clothes. He kissed her hand lingeringly and left without a word.

She had a quick shower and donned her disguise.

'Dot, ask Mr. B. to get me the officer in charge of the dock case. He's Constable Collins' superior and I've forgotten his name.'

Mr. Butler, having seen Peter Smith out and shut the front door, lifted the receiver and asked for Russell Street Police Station.

Dot came up, with both girls, eager to find out how the night had gone.

'Well, Miss, did you find out anything?'

'Yes. Lots of things. Some to the purpose. I have to go into the city, Dot, and meet an anarchist woman. How do I look?'

'Awful,' said Jane, candidly. Ruth nodded.

'Good. Full of political consciousness and no time for fashion. Now, I'll be back as soon as I can. Be good, ladies, and don't forget to go and collect the diary from Mary Tachell. And if you can help it, don't affront the poor little thing. She's not very attractive and not very clever and without one of those her future is likely to be dire. All right?'

They nodded solemnly. Phryne ran down the stairs, hoping that she was not corrupting her two adoptive daughters too badly, and reflecting that she really must remember her audience when minded to coin aphorisms.

'She's lovely,' said Jane, affectionately. 'But she's terribly cynical.'

Ruth agreed. 'I suppose that all grown-ups are like that.'

'You can go and clean up your room,' snapped Dot. 'And mind your language about Miss Phryne. If it hadn't been for her you two would still be slaveys in a boarding house.'

Subdued, they raced down the stairs to make beds, and play games with Ember, who regarded all housework as a challenge to his ingenuity.

◇◇◇

The policeman sounded wary on the telephone, but not hostile.

'Yes, Miss Fisher, I have heard of you. Detective-Inspector Robinson speaks very highly of you. I'll help you if I can. I do understand, as an old digger, how you feel about being shot at.'

'Good. I'm told a young woman is coming to identify my dead young man this morning.'

'That is correct. She gave her name as Mary Evans.'

'And you believe that?'

'She didn't sound like any Evans I ever heard,' he admitted. 'Balt, I reckon.'

'I would like to come along to the morgue with you.'

'If you like, Miss Fisher. As long as it isn't in any official capacity, you understand.'

'Not at all. I am anxious to be wholly unofficial. When is she expected?'

'Ten-thirty.'

'Oh, Lord, can you delay her until I come?'

'If you can come soon.'

'I'll drive like the wind,' Phryne promised, and hung up on the remonstrance about speed limits which he felt that he had to make.

Mr. Butler took to The Esplanade with a roar, and whisked Phryne into the city in twenty minutes. He dropped her outside the police station and drove carefully down Russell Street to a pub where he could repair his nerve. He had not driven that fast in his life before.

Phryne, drab as a sparrow, enquired for Detective-Sergeant Carroll and was directed into the bowels of the building, where she promptly got lost and had to be rescued by a passing cadet.

She knocked, and a gruff voice ordered her to enter.

In the small cupboard allotted to this guardian of the law a very large police officer was wedged, in company with a thin pale girl bowed under the weight of a sheaf of brown hair which had, recently, been dyed black. She looked up at Phryne's entry and revealed a face of such naked sorrow that Phryne flinched.

'Ah, there you are, where have you been? Got lost? Come on, Miss Evans. Now we got someone to support you. Off we go.' He twitched the thin girl up from her chair and thrust her out into the corridor. 'Collins!' he roared, 'take these ladies to the morgue and get an identification for your dead 'un, then come back here. There's been a baby discovered in the river.'

Constable Collins took the girl's arm, recognized Phryne, opened his mouth to make an unwise declaration, then shut it again under the impetus of Phryne's forty-watt glare. The girl sagged on Collins' arm and he bore her up with some anxiety.

'Come along, my dear,' said Phryne, taking the other arm. 'This is very brave of you. You know that he would have wanted you to be brave.'

The wounded eyes, drowned in dark shadows, stared into her face. Phryne was almost painfully reminded of the blazing eyes of her lover of the night before, and melted at the knees. She dug her fingernails into her palm and returned the gaze.

'Who are you?' asked a thready voice. Phryne had not prepared an alias, and grasped at her French Apache name.

'I am *La Chatte Noire*, and Peter sent me to support you.'

'Peter...'

'Peter Smith.' She touched her collarbone, and the young woman appeared satisfied. Mary Evans leaned her weight on Collins as he led them out into the courtyard and handed them into a police car, climbing into the front.

The morgue was a depressing brick building which could not really be anything else. The sun however shone brightly, and Phryne wished that her part did not require her to wear black. Collins escorted them into the cold chamber, stinking of disinfectant, and an attendant wheeled out the body, draped in a sheet and naked as the day he was born.

Phryne looked as Mary stared; she could not avoid it. He seemed serene, now, cleansed of mud; the hair had dried flossy, like silk.

'Glad you've come,' remarked the attendant, a fat young man with greasy hair and a serious complexion problem. 'We can't keep all the corpses we find, you know. Pretty soon Coroner would refuse to sit on him.'

Collins, who had not got used to death, turned on him in a fury.

'You shut that mouth, you ratbag,' he snapped, and the attendant blanched so that his pimples stood out like lanterns.

'All right, boss, no need to get shirty,' he stammered.

'Is this man known to you, Miss?' asked Collins formally.

Mary Evans nodded tremulously.

'What is his name?'

'Yourka. His name is Yourka Rosen.'

'All right, Miss. Sign the form. Full name and address, please.'

Mary reached out a thin hand reddened with housework and touched the cheek. The coldness of the dead struck such a chill through her that Phryne felt it through her embrace, and bore Mary up as she collapsed.

'Take him away,' she ordered, and the attendant rolled the trolley out, Phryne hoping vengefully that acne was a terminal condition. Mary sat up on the floor, and signed Collins' form.

She gave her address as the Great Southern Private Hotel and began to sign her name with an A before she remembered that her name was Evans. She spoke in French, to Phryne.

'Will he be buried in the Church? I have no money to bury him!' She wailed and rocked in unappeasable grief, and Phryne stood up and addressed the constable.

'Nothing you can do here, Collins, go back to Russell Street. And give that pimply necrophile the news that I will pay for a proper Catholic funeral and he'd better make sure that the body is suitably dealt with. All right?'

'Yes, Miss,' stammered Collins, and left to over-awe the front office, profoundly glad to be out of this chill room smelling of death.

Mary was weeping distractedly, and Phryne let her cry for ten minutes before she drew her to her feet and walked her out of the room.

'We must get out of here,' said Phryne, escorting the woman into Batman Avenue. The river glinted through the trees and Phryne saw the Melbourne Boat House, scene of many wild parties. The balcony, against all likelihood, was still defying gravity.

Mary moved like a sleepwalker, weeping distractedly, as they staggered past the swimming pool with its dolphins and sun-bathers waving from the roof.

'Down this track,' Phryne decided, crossing Prince's Bridge and descending to the bare track which ran along the river. 'Do calm yourself, Mary!'

Crying so convulsively that her body shook in Phryne's embrace, Mary negotiated the steps and they continued along the river, which was full and looked sullen and very cold. Small boats passed on their way to Queen's wharf. Ahead, past the railway bridge, was the clutter of brick warehouses under the line, where Phryne hoped to obtain some tea in relative obscurity.

Under the Sandridge line and near to the wharf they stopped. There was a pie cart. Phryne dragged Mary up the sloping bank and onto the shore, sat her down on a brick wall and rummaged for some money.

'Two teas, please,' she said, to the unshaven personage presiding over the urn, which leaked and hissed steam. 'No, on second thought, one tea.'

'What's wrong, lady, don't you fancy my tea?' asked the pie-cart proprietor, grinning with all of his remaining teeth.

'No,' agreed Phryne. 'I don't. Now we've just come from the morgue and I don't feel like trading comic cross-talk with you. Tea, and look slippy.'

'Oh, been to the morgue, eh? I'll put a slug in it, then. The poor sheila. Husband?'

'Cousin. Thank you. What is it?'

He held up the bottle. 'Navy Rum.'

'That will do nicely.' Phryne paid him a shilling for the tea, loaded it with sugar and took it back to Mary. She waved it away, then accepted it as Phryne shoved the cup into her hand. The pie-cart owner had been generous with his rum. Phryne could smell the raw alcoholic vapour from two feet away.

Mary sipped, sniffed, then sipped again, seeming surprised at the taste.

She had stopped crying.

'He is dead,' she whispered. 'All along I had hoped that it was not Yourka that they had killed. But it was Yourka,' she added. 'He is dead and he is my last cousin. The Revolution has killed them all.' She took a gulp of the scalding tea. 'Have some,' she offered, and Phryne decided to give the pie-cart owner his chance. She obtained another cup and was astonished to find that it was good, though strong. A dray lumbered past on what seemed to be elliptical wheels, the horses straining at the collar. She waved away the dung-laden dust and sat down on the wall next to Mary again.

'There is nothing that I can do for Yourka now. Being dead. But I am still alive and I can revenge him.'

'Can you?'

'Of course. I know all their plans. They killed him because he was young and stupid. Do you know how old Yourka was?'

'No.'

'Seventeen. And now he will never be eighteen. The dead are forever young, forever beautiful. *Chatte Noire*, did you not think him beautiful? As a comrade, I sleep with all of them, but Yourka was my cousin and my lover. So gentle, so young. His flesh was my delight. When I touched him just then death had turned him to stone. Cold as moss. I will revenge him,' she added, simply.

Phryne patted her hand, at a loss for a comment. Her use of English was as stark as scripture. Cold as moss. So he had been, poor Yourka.

'I shall bury him in the church,' she said at length. 'Who was your priest?'

'Father Reilly, at Our Lady Star of the Sea, bless you!'

Mary launched herself into Phryne's arms and kissed her moistly.

'The comrades must not know.'

'Not know what?'

'That he will be buried in the church. They do not believe in God. They do not allow anyone else to believe in God, either, though that did not stop Yourka from believing. He used to pray his little child's prayer every night, because he knew no other. I shall miss him for the rest of my life, which will not be long if they catch me talking to you.'

'Why?'

'Because Peter sent you. I like Peter, I have known him all my life, but the others do not respect him, even though he has grown old in the struggle. He is against their *illégalisme*. He says that it will make Australia into a police state, which is true. They will not accept this. I do not know who you are, *ma Chatte*, but you are a friend of Peter's or he would not have sent you, he must trust you, therefore they will not.'

'That makes sense.'

'But I like you and I owe you a debt for burying Yourka in God, which is all I can do for him now. I should have warned him. I did not, because I thought they would not kill him. But they killed him,' she said, sadly. 'Shall we have more tea?'

Phryne ordered more tea, bemused.

'However, first I must consult the spirits.'

'The spirits?'

'Indeed. We go to Madame Stella, who is Jean Vassileva, she holds seances at the Socialist Bookshop in Spencer Street every Tuesday night. They, and I, have always been given good advice by the spirits. They always take her advice. They get in touch with the old dead anarchists through her, and Lenin.'

'Lenin?'

'Vladimir Ilyich Ulyanov, the Russian leader, you must have heard of him.'

'Of course, but I have never spoken to him,' said Phryne. 'May I come too?'

'Of course. The spirits are there for all. Now I must go. They do not know that I have identified Yourka, and they must not know. I will see you at the seance, *ma Chatte*. Eight o'clock, in an upstairs room at the Bookshop. God bless you,' and she was gone, moving slowly as though she was carrying a heavy weight on her shoulders, the long black hair spraying dull across her black-clad back.

Phryne went to the Socialist Bookshop and Tearoom—the house of all the red-raggers in Melbourne—and asked for Jean Vassileva. The plump lady behind the counter paused to sell a pamphlet on Spain and chirped.

'She's sitting over there, dear! If you want tomorrow's seance it's one pound a ticket. You can buy them from me.'

'One ticket, please.'

Phryne handed across her one quid and then walked over to a well-dressed middle-aged woman who was eating bread and butter and looked just like a Fitzroy housewife.

'Hello! I hear that you are in contact with the spirits.'

'All is known in the other world, dearie,' said Jean in a broad Australian accent. 'Got your ticket? I can't do with a big crowd, you see, because the Guide don't like it.'

'The Guide?'

'Bright Feather, me spirit guide. He's in charge. What are you looking for, eh? Lost someone?'

She was eyeing the black dress avidly. This woman could not be a real medium, Phryne decided, and was exactly the person she was looking for.

'You have some strange customers,' she commented. 'Anarchists and foreigners and all.'

Jean gave her a frightened glance and muttered, 'They scare me to death, dearie, I don't mind bloody telling you. Even though me old man is Latvian. I had to learn the lingo to tell me mum-in-law what I thought of her. But they pay well, the red-raggers.'

'You're a fake, aren't you?'

'Most of the time, dear, yes. The spirits do come, you know, but the customers want a result every time. They will want their money back if I don't produce little Tommy who died on the Front. Though there's not so many of them any more,' she reflected. 'Forgotten or passed on, I expect. What's it to you?'

'I want to visit your seance without being identified,' said Phryne, passing Jean a ten pound note.

'The spirits are at your disposal, dearie.'

Chapter Seven

'There is no honour among thieves.'

Proverb

'Reckon we've drawn a blank, mate,' sighed Cec, setting down his fifth pot with care. His extremities became unreliable after the fifth.

'Yair, mate, I reckon we might as well turn it up for today. Monday's never a good day for the crims. They're all recuperating from the weekend.'

Bert and Cec were tired and more than a little drunk. They had enquired assiduously but cautiously through all the pubs where Melbourne criminals were wont to carouse and so far had drawn a complete blank. They were now refreshing their strength in their favourite pub, Markillies, while waiting for fresh inspiration.

They finished their drinks and were in the process of getting up when a quiet voice commented, 'I hear you've been asking some questions, Bert.'

'Yair, Billy, we have,' Bert replied, sitting down with his hands on the table, where they could be seen. Little Billy Ferguson was the associate and hired killer of most of Melbourne's more unpleasant gangs, had several murders to his debit, and was, in popular opinion, 'as mad as a cut snake.' He was known to be the minder for Happy Harry's two-up school, and several policemen had sworn to get him, only to meet with unforeseen misadventures. Physically, Billy Ferguson was small, thin, and softly spoken. No one would have noticed him in a crowd. He was one of the few men of whom both Bert and Cec were afraid.

'What do you want to know, and why?'

'We're working for that lady detective, Miss Fisher. Someone shot at her outside the dock gates on Sat'dy and she don't take to being shot at. She wants to know who did it.'

'I see. Now, I might know who did it, if you promise not to keep poking your noses into my business.'

'Honest, Billy, we never knew it was any of your business or we wouldn't even have asked.'

'It ain't none of my business,' snapped Billy, sending a chill through Cec. Billy was always armed. 'The name of the criminals is written on this bit of paper. Here. They're giving crime a bad name, they are. They're commos. You're a commo, ain't yer?'

'Yair, Billy, I am,' agreed Bert, wondering if he was about to join the glorious company of martyrs of the Revolution. Billy grinned unpleasantly.

'Then you oughta be able to find 'em, and if you need any help with 'em, you can call on me. Bastards, all of 'em. See you, Bert, Cec. You won't ask no more questions, will yer?'

'No, Billy, no more questions at all.'

Billy walked out of the pub. Drinkers shifted out of his path. Bert wiped his brow and opened the betting slip.

'Max Dubof and Karl Smoller,' he said aloud. 'I hope this'll be enough for her.'

'Too right,' said Cec.

◇◇◇

Phryne had ordered chocolate—she would not be able to face tea for quite a while—in the tea rooms of Russell Collins, which was chic, and a change from the Socialist Bookshop.

She was reviewing the next two days and wondering how she was going to fit it all in. At least she was free tonight, and could put herself to bed early in preparation for Tuesday night. Pity about the ballet.

The problem of the tattoo arose in her mind. How to produce a waterproof blue anarchist tattoo, without permanently marking her skin? She finished the chocolate and visited the Ladies' Room, which was appropriately opulent, paying the bill on the way out.

With a wave she summoned a taxi and ordered a puzzled driver to take her to the Professor's tattoo salon, next to Antonio's Hotel in Flinders Street.

The driver uttered not a word, though he was later to add it to his collection of 'my most unforgettable fares.'

The tattoo salon was brightly lit, lined with celluloid templates stained with various inks, and rather full of gaping men.

It was a full minute before any of the inhabitants moved, and even then they just shifted their gaze. One removed a cigarette.

The skinny boy, scanning the full-rigged ship which he intended to have decorating his arm as soon as the Professor could be induced to accept a note from his father, grinned cheekily and asked, 'What can we do for you, Miss?'

'You can introduce me to the Professor,' replied Phryne, and the boy ran a hand through his curly red hair and called: 'Professor! Lady to see you!'

He then returned to his contemplation of the templates. Perhaps a black cat would be better. The Professor would never notice that the permission was not in his father's writing.

A large man put down his needle and emptied his glass of beer. 'Yes, Miss? Want a tattoo, do you?'

Phryne ignored the laughter and said coolly, 'I want a transfer. I remember that when I was a child one could produce an ink picture on the skin. I do not want a permanent tattoo. Can you do it?'

The Professor removed his hat and scratched his head, where the black hair was thinning.

'You don't know what you are asking,' he complained. 'My skill is with the needle. I don't do transfers.'

'How permanent is your ink?'

'My ink lasts forever. You'll go to your grave with one of my tats.'

'I see. And is it waterproof?'

'Yair, but once it's under the skin it don't have to be. You can't wash off skin.'

'And how do you mark the design?'

'Like this.' He reached for a template, inked it with a roller, and curved the inked side around his own arm. He peeled the celluloid off with great skill and left on his skin the reverse of the picture scratched on the template.

'See? I don't do freehand drawings. Illustrations, that's what they are. Some of them come from America.'

'But you could make one?'

'Sure.'

Phryne produced her design. The Professor took a square of celluloid and carved the design into it.

'There you are, lady. Now, since you don't want a tat, I must ask you to leave.'

'Oh, no, you don't, I need the right coloured ink. You can apply it, if you please. I will pay a standard fee.'

'Whatever you say. What colour?'

'Blue.'

He inked the template and gestured Phryne to a chair, beside another sufferer at whose arm she did not like to look. It was a mess of ink and blood and must have been very painful.

'Where do you want this?' asked the Professor resignedly, approaching with the template. Phryne unbuttoned the drab dress and exposed her cleavage.

'Oh, cripes no!' he recoiled. Phryne was firm.

'Come on, now, be a brave Professor. Just here, if you please, and don't smudge.'

Averting his eyes, the Professor applied the template with unstudied efficiency, peeled it off. The circled capital A was as clear as print and definitively blue.

'Good. How long does it take to dry?'

'Ten minutes,' gasped the Professor, who had only applied such decorations to ladies of very light repute indeed. His present client did not fall into that class and he found her very disturbing. She, however, was as cool as a halibut on ice and was chatting in a social tone, holding her dress apart so as not to touch the ink.

'Have you seen that design before? Oh, do go on with your work,' she offered generously. 'I would not like to interrupt you.' The news of what was happening in the tattoo salon had emptied the pub. More drinkers crammed into the shop, until Phryne found it difficult to breathe and the Professor was forced to clear the place with a full-throated roar which drove them onto the street again. The crowd attracted Bert and Cec, who took one look into the salon and ducked out again.

'You reckon we should wait for her, mate?' asked Cec. Bert nodded.

'There might be trouble.' He took up his post leaning against the wall. 'So we stay.'

'No, I never seen that design before,' answered the Professor, concentrating on the arm in front of him and wiping blood away with cotton wool. 'There you are, son.'

The patient managed a grin and smiled across at Phryne.

'It don't hurt much,' he lied. 'Why not give it a go?'

The Professor groaned, but Phryne answered collectedly, 'Not today. I'll think about it.'

'That'll be dry now, Miss. It will last about a week, and then it'll wash off. And be nice, Miss, *don't* think about it. You don't want a tattoo. You don't want to go spoiling them nice…I mean, you really don't want one. It ain't right for a lady. That'll be five bob,' he added, grossly overcharging to compensate for having his afternoon ruined. 'And thank you.' He ushered Phryne out, enquired politely of the gathered drinkers as to whether they had any homes to go to, and retreated into his salon, mopping his brow.

The red-headed kid had decided on the ship. The Professor did not even glance at the letter from his father. The boy felt rather hurt. He had gone to a lot of trouble to forge it.

◇◇◇

'Need a lift home, lady?' asked Bert, and Phryne turned to demolish him, paused in mid-word, and took his arm.

'Why, thank you,' she smiled, and the assembled drinkers muttered with envy.

Safe in the taxi, Phryne lit a gasper and expelled the breath which she had been holding.

'Have you got any tattoos, Bert?'

'Yair.'

'I don't know how you stood it. Talk about mutilation. What a place!'

'That's the anarchist tat, eh? Clever of you to think of it, Miss, and brave of you to go into the Professor's den.'

'No, not at all, poor man, he was very polite.'

'Yair, well, he ain't used to ladies coming into his salon. We found out who shot the boy, Miss, and who shot at you.'

'You did? Bert, that's wonderful!'

'We were told,' Bert admitted. 'Little Billy Ferguson gave us the office. We'd been asking questions, see, and he don't approve of people asking questions. A bad man, Miss. You got that betting slip, Cec?'

Cec handed Phryne the grubby paper. She tucked it into her purse.

'That's excellent work, Bert, really excellent, and so quick! What's wrong with Little Billy?'

'Nothing, if you like murderers, and I don't. He's got them pale blue eyes that look straight through yer. Give a man the grues, he would.'

'Does he give you the grues, Cec?'

'You bet, Miss.'

'An impressively nasty character, evidently. Were you in any danger?'

'Nah, he don't like the commos, he says that the anarchists are giving crime a bad name. Wasn't it Little Billy that did for that cop outside the Olympic Games pub?'

Cec nodded.

'Olympic Games? I don't know a hotel of that name.'

'Nah, it's called the Railway Hotel. In 'Roy. They have an SP in the courtyard, see, and when the cops raid 'em there's lots of Olympic events for the blokes who are running away. The long jump, the hundred yard dash, the high-jump over the wall.'

Phryne laughed.

'Home, Miss? And you got anything more for us to do?'

'Not at the moment. I'll call you if I need you. Thanks for the ride, friends. How much?'

'On the house,' said Bert, chuckling. 'You've done me a bit of good at Antonio's. No one expected me to pick up the best-looking sheila in Flinders Street. Give us a call if you need us, Miss. Good night.'

Phryne was met with downcast looks from both girls and Dot when she breezed in.

'Whatever is the matter? Had bad news?'

'It's Mary Tachell, Miss,' explained Dot. 'We telephoned her house and her mother says that she's come down with a bilious attack and won't be up for a week.'

'Little beast. She ate like a pig!' muttered Ruth.

'Never mind. One thing about investigation, my dears, is that where one avenue closes, another opens. I now know who killed Yourka Rosen (that is the young man's name) and I am going to a seance tomorrow night to do a little...er...manipulation of his murderers. So I can't go to the ballet, girls, but never mind; you shall go regardless. I must get out of this depressing dress. Excuse me. Oh, Mr. Butler, put on all the alarms tonight. We might have visitors. Has anyone called?'

'Mr. Smith, Miss. He will call again. No one else.'

'Good,' and Phryne floated up the stairs to a wash and a rest.

◇◇◇

Phryne spent a blameless evening reading *The Winter's Tale* with Ruth, who was still convinced that Shakespeare could bear translation.

'Why does he take so long to say anything?'

'The Elizabethan stage had no scenes and only hand-props. His actors had to create the scene, as well as the action. Look how cleverly he has leafed the innocent conversation of the Queen and Polixenes with the King's own jealous thoughts. It works very well onstage, I promise. We shall go to the next Shakespeare anyone puts on. You shall see.'

'But they are like brothers, it's explained in the first scene,' objected Ruth. 'How could he possibly get such a wrong idea?'

'There is no sense in jealousy, pet, and no King or brotherhood is proof against a bee in the bonnet.'

'I suppose so,' agreed Ruth, and kept reading.

Altogether it was a very agreeable evening and Phryne put herself to bed full of remembered love and poetry.

◇◇◇

Tuesday dawned clear and cool with promise of sun to come, and Phryne remembered her tattoo in the nick of time and washed around it. She made an experimental dab with the sponge and no ink came off.

Phryne occupied her morning with an extensive telephone canvass of all the girls at the convent and the Presbyterian Ladies College to whom Alicia Waddington-Forsythe could possibly have fled. Reverend Mother provided the convent girls, and Jane the PLC. None of them had seen her, and most of them seemed relieved that they had not. She laid down the phone at eleven, found her bathing costume, and went out to the beach for a brief swim. She hoped the bracing water would help her think.

Phryne knew that bathing was tolerated, though strictly illegal, on St. Kilda beach during the hours between sunrise and sunset, and had bought her costume in Paris. It had no legs and very little back and she was somewhat disappointed that there was no one on the beach to be shocked by her semi-nakedness. This would test the tattoo, she thought, and plunged forward into the sea, which closed, salt and bitter, over her head.

It was while she was returning, glowing and shivering by turns, that a blanket was thrown over her head and she was seized by strong arms.

The blanket was sandy and she began to choke, kicked wildly, and felt one of her heels sink into something soft. Gaining her advantage, she shot out both hands and grabbed.

Although she could not see what she had seized, it was evidently a part which her assailant valued. She heard a howl, and the arms slackened their grip.

Phryne tightened her fingers. The arms fell away, and someone began flailing at her blanket-covered head, swearing in an unknown language. Phryne shook herself and the blanket slipped.

She had chosen her hold well. The parts of the man she had clawed into a bundle were those which gave him the designation, and he exhibited every sign of wanting them back.

Phryne let go, tripped him, and knelt on his chest as he wept hot tears and clutched at his organs.

'You bastard, who are you? What do you want with me? Talk, or I'll tear them off with my teeth!' she hissed, red-faced and furious and spitting sand.

'No!' he cried. 'I was only obeying orders!'

'Whose orders?'

This, even at the threat to his manhood, he would not answer.

'Tell your boss,' said Phryne with measured loathing, 'that I will speak to him or I will meet him, but the next fool he sends within my grasp I will castrate with a blunt knife. Repeat it.' It took three attempts for the blubbering attacker to learn this threat off by heart and then Phryne jumped off him and backed three paces.

'I'd go now, if I were you,' she said, conversationally. He understood her quickly. He ran away down the beach, and Phryne walked back into the sea to wash his touch and the sand off her body.

Trembling with reaction, she found her beach pyjamas, re-clothed herself and walked back to her house. Not a young man, perhaps forty, heavy Slavic accent, greying hair, forgettable face. She had, in fact, not really looked at his face.

Perhaps I should not have let him go. Perhaps next time they will just shoot me. But he wanted me alive, that was a kidnapping attempt, thought Phryne, ringing her own doorbell. And what would I have done with him? What with Ember and Jane and Ruthie and Mr. and Mrs. Butler and me, it's becoming a rather full house. I should have looked for the car. Never mind. I wonder how the tattoo stood up to all that? I wouldn't like to have to bother the Professor again.

She peered down her front. The anarchist brand was still there, a little paler, but seemingly indelible.

'Did you have a nice swim, Miss Fisher?' Mr. Butler opened the door. Phryne smiled seraphically.

'Thank you, Mr. Butler, it was most congenial.'

Chapter Eight

'...I am angling now,
Though you perceive me not how I give line.'
William Shakespeare, *The Winter's Tale*

Phryne ran up to her boudoir and shut herself in. She was trembling all over with shock and rage, and she had broken a fingernail and bruised one shin. She flung herself down on her bed and closed her eyes, willing the fury to drain out of her before it shook her to pieces.

So easily caught! If there had been more than one of them I would have been taken, without clothes, without weapons. Not again. I go armed even in the bath and the Lord protect whoever touches me!

It had been an anarchist, she was sure. Perhaps it had been one of the two names she had been given. If so, he would now be mourning seriously twisted testicles. Yourka Rosen was already a little avenged. This thought made her chuckle, and she felt better. Then she ran straight to her bathroom and was luxuriously sick.

This completed her cure. She brushed her teeth, poured a small Laphroaig, took a cool shower, and washed all the sand out of her hair. By the time she was sitting down at her mirror and cutting the affronted nail Dot was tapping at the door.

'Miss? Miss Phryne? Are you all right?'

'Come in, Dot. I'm fine. Some son of unmarried parents just tried to kidnap me.'

'What did you do with the body, Miss?' Dot was calm. 'Was this on the beach? Only one of them?'

'Yes, on the beach, he threw a blanket over my head, but I managed to persuade him to drop me.' Phryne suppressed any communication on the method used, in deference to her maid's modesty. 'And then I let him go, blast it.'

'Lucky, too.' Dot took up the scissors and began to trim the nail. 'What would you do with him? I mean, apart from mulch.'

'Dot, I believe that I have corrupted you.'

'Me, Miss? I don't care what happens to someone who shoots at you!' Dot replaced the scissors in their case.

'Are you looking forward to the ballet? What are you going to wear?'

'Yes, Miss, I've never been to the ballet before, though I wish that you were coming too. I'm going to wear the dark-brown figured velvet and the orangey cloche with the velvet flowers.'

'Yes, that will do very well. And you need a coat. Take the green one, that won't clash. Your blue will not match at all.'

'Thank you, Miss. That will look nice. Mr. Peter Smith rang, Miss. He said he'd call back at two.'

'Good. Now I'm going to sleep, Dot, and I don't want to be woken except for an emergency. Wake me at half-past one with a light lunch and ask the girls to forgive me for not going to the beach with them. No one is going anywhere, Dot. Tell them what happened and allow them to invite their friends here, if they like. Imagine what would have happened if it had been you, or Ruthie or Jane.'

'Them two can look after themselves,' muttered Dot. 'I'll tell 'em. Let me find you a nightdress, Miss, and I'll tuck you up. There you are. Sleep well. No one won't go out, and if anyone tries to come in they will be sorry.'

Dot went out, closing the door with a quiet click, and stalked down the stairs, calling for Phryne's daughters. They were emerging from their room clad in bathing costumes more decorous than Phryne's.

'When are we going out?' asked Ruth.

'We ain't. Someone just made an attempt to kidnap Miss Phryne. She says no one is to go out but you can invite anyone in.'

'Gosh! How is the poor man?'

'He ran away,' Dot smiled. 'And I should think so, too. It's these revolutionaries. We never ought to have got mixed up with them. Who would you like to invite to lunch?'

Both girls thought hard.

'What about Estelle Underwood?' suggested Ruth, but Jane objected. 'She'll bring her soppy brother with her.'

'Yes, I know,' said Ruth patiently. 'And he goes to school with Alicia Waddington-Forsythe's brother.'

'You know, Ruthie, you are sometimes almost intelligent,' said Jane, ducking Ruth's slap. Dot smiled on them.

'That's a good pair of girls to try and help Miss Phryne. But be careful. She always says that the big danger in investigation is saying too much.'

'We'll be careful,' promised Ruth, and went down the hall to obtain the number of Estelle Underwood and her soppy brother.

◇◇◇

Phryne slept peacefully through the advent of Rupert and Estelle Underwood, who were pleased to condescend to eating Mrs. Butler's lunch and required no prompting to talk about the Waddington-Forsythes.

'Oh, yes, Paul was distraught when his sister went missing. Some lady rang Mother yesterday, asking if we had seen her.'

'And had you?' asked Jane idly, passing the cream cakes. Jane had eaten more cream cakes in the last two days than she had previously believed existed, and was now able to regard them with only a languid interest.

'No! Paul has been to visit, of course. Poor fellow. He's desperately in love with his stepmother, you know. Quite a pash. She's twenty-five, though, far too old for him.'

'Practically antique,' agreed his sister. 'But I don't think that you are fair to Alicia. She's a very good sort of girl, very religious. She was always talking about the convent and how she wanted to be a nun. She would have made a good nun and her father dragged her out of the sisterhood, where she was happy, and pushed her into school, and then she turned into a beastly little prig. Bound to happen. Why does her father want her to make a good marriage, anyway? Positively prehistoric.'

'Aren't you going to get married, Estelle?'

'Yes, I hope so, but it won't be because my father wants me to.'

'I don't think Paul is likely to marry,' commented Rupert. 'He's always talking about perfect love and that sort of thing. Reads Ruskin. Like me, he wants to burn with a hard, gem-like flame and you can't do that if you are married and have a lot of brats and nurseries and all that sordid mess.'

Rupert had never forgiven his mother for continuing to have children once she had achieved the heights of human creation by giving birth to Rupert. He was, however, particularly fond of his sister, whose uncompromising plainness made a good foil for his Pre-Raphaelite beauty. He looked rather alarmingly like his friend Paul. He stretched out his legs and leaned back. He approved of Miss Fisher's salon. He liked the pair of full-length nudes which decorated the main wall. 'La Source,' a female holding an amphora on her shoulder from which water flowed, and 'Poseidon,' where the river ended in the sea, nude and lightly muscled, crowned with seaweed. He was toying with the idea of following in the divine Oscar's footsteps and found his friend's fascination with his stepmother both puzzling and faintly disgusting.

'What does Paul say about her?' asked Ruth, artlessly. 'Doesn't he think that she's too old?'

'He says that she looks just like the Blessed Damozel, leaning out from the gold bar of Heaven,' replied Rupert. 'I can't see it myself. I don't like her, to be candid. Doe eyes and all a-tremble if you make a noise or drop something. And she is...she is...'

'Expecting,' said his sister, practically.

'Yes, that. You could not find a lady in that…unfortunate condition attractive.'

Jane glanced at Ruth. Rupert was soppy, there was no denying it.

'Of course, you probably don't understand what I mean,' condescended Rupert. 'Being girls. Love can only be understood properly by a masculine mind.'

Ordinarily that would have earned Rupert an impressive set of retributions, including a beating with cushions, but Jane and Ruth had sterner aims and were not to be distracted.

'Oh, indeed? Tell us, then.'

'I say, you can't understand it unless you are a chap and I don't know that I like to talk about it to a lot of girls,' objected Rupert. 'I mean, you haven't got the same…er…passions.'

'Haven't we?' asked Jane artlessly, thinking of Phryne. 'I don't think that you are right, Rupert. Come on. What did Paul tell you about his stepmother?'

'Do tell us!' urged Ruth.

His sister added, 'Come on, Rupert, you can't torment us like this. If you know anything, spit it out! Or else shut up about it.'

'Oh, all right.' Rupert took a cake, crossly. 'He said—mind you, this is just what he *said*, that doesn't mean I believe it…'

'Oh, come on Rupert, have a heart,' groaned Ruth, flinging a cushion, which he fended off his cake with ease.

'He said that she had allowed him…had allowed him to… er…you know.'

'No, I don't know and if I did I would not be asking you!' exclaimed Jane, whose education in matters sexual had been full and informative but short on euphemisms. Rupert blushed red and ran a distracted hand through his hair.

'I mean that she had given him the ultimate favour.'

There was silence in the room.

'Gosh,' said Jane, lamely.

'Yes,' agreed Rupert.

'Good Lord defend us!' exclaimed Dot silently from the kitchen door, where she stood frozen to the spot with a teapot unregarded in her hand. She only noticed it when she was minded to cross herself.

'I think we should go and play some records,' said Jane, and they retired to the girls' room to wind up the gramophone, which had been a present from a policeman called Jack Robinson. The strains of a jazz song could be heard through the door.

> 'It ain't gonna rain no more no more,
> It ain't gonna rain no more!
> How in the heck can I wash my neck
> If it ain't gonna rain no more?'

Phryne woke, relaxed and warm, to take the tray from Dot and eat her boiled egg in comfort. Dot sat down on the edge of the bed to wait for the tray. Phryne noticed that Dot was pale and seemed shocked.

'What's happened? Has there been an attack?'

'No, Miss, we're safe as houses. It's something the girls have found out, but I'll leave it to them to tell you. After all, they discovered it.'

'If it is that the repulsive Paul is sleeping with his stepmother, I've guessed it already. It still does not help us to discover Alicia. I wonder where the little pest is? She might never have left the convent, you know. Mother Superior may be practising "economy of truth."'

'She ain't a Jesuit, Miss, she's an Anglican. I don't think they have it.'

'You didn't think they had convents. I need that awful black dress again for tonight, but now I feel like being magnificent. Give me the silver and jade lounging robe and my pantoufles. Are the girls' visitors still here?'

'Yes, Miss.'

'What's the time?'

'Two o'clock, Miss.'

'Good. I'll stay here and wait for Mr. Smith's call. Don't worry, Dot. Dismiss it from your mind. We'll find the little beast. And the perversions of the sins of the flesh are not confined to the working class, you know.'

'It's a shock, though.'

Dot went out, shaking her head, with the tray.

The call came exactly at the promised time, and Phryne picked up her own telephone and said, 'Thank you, Mr. B., I'll take the call.'

The voice was low and urgent.

'Phryne, I hear that bad things have happened.'

'Unsuccessfully.'

'You escaped?'

'They never held on to me.'

Peter chuckled, a deep, rich laugh.

'I said that you were unique.'

'Thank you.'

'But they will try again.'

'I expect so, but I shall be prepared. They will be very sorry that they tried. But they don't want me dead or they could have shot me as I stood. Don't worry.'

'When shall I see you again?'

'Come on Wednesday night. Come to dinner,' said Phryne, who knew the way to this man's heart. 'About seven-thirty.'

'I will be there, and so, I hope, will you.'

'You can rely on it,' said Phryne, and rang off.

Since there was nothing else to do until later, she lay back in her big chair in her glittering gown and watched the sea, and the ships which crossed it from one horizon to another. She always found the sea soothing.

◇◇◇

Dot and the girls were dressed in their new clothes and sent off with Mr. Butler in the Hispano-Suiza. They would pick up Dr. MacMillan on the way. Phryne was clad in her old black dress, over which she was wearing a ratty overcoat which Mr. Butler wore when changing tyres on wet days. She had damaged a perfectly good felt hat in producing the correct secondhand droop, immersing it firmly in her bath and drying it in the spring sun.

Bert and Cec arrived in their cab, whistled derisively when they saw her attire, and headed for the city.

'You want us to wait, Miss?'

'Yes. Somewhere out of sight. Round the corner, perhaps, in one of those lanes. I'm armed and I feel fairly safe, but they have already tried to kidnap me today.'

'They tried a snatch on you, Miss?'

'Yes. It did not succeed, as you can tell. If I appear escorted or carried, follow and find out where they are taking me, but give me at least three hours before you do anything. I want to have both of these men hanged, and I am willing to risk a bit of discomfort for that. If I'm not out within three hours, come and get me. The cop in charge of the case is Detective-Sergeant Bill Carroll. But don't wait until he turns up. I leave it to your discretion. Here we are, Bert. Stop here. I shall walk the rest of the way.'

'Good luck,' said Bert. He steered the car around the corner and turned into a dark and noisome lane.

'All we need is some nosy copper moving us on,' he growled. Cec peered into the night.

'No one in sight, mate. How about a smoke?'

Bert accepted the pouch and began to roll a cigarette. He did not like waiting.

◇◇◇

Phryne huddled into the coat. She had received the girls' revelations with gratitude, and had thanked them for their excellent efforts on her behalf. She had leapt to the conclusion that the beautiful Paul had been conducting some sort of affair with Christine, and it was pleasing to have her suspicions confirmed, but it gave her no clue to the disappearance of Alicia. Where could she be? Had she left the convent? Had she gone home again? If so, she had not seen her father.

Meanwhile, there were the anarchists. Phryne was wearing her Beretta in her garter, and she had a throwing knife strapped to her forearm. She did not intend to be taken by surprise again.

The Socialist Bookshop was closed but she knocked at the door and a thin, dark young man let her in. The bookshelves, stuffed with literature, loomed dark and indistinct. The young man took Phryne's hand and led her up half-seen stairs into a large chamber hung with black cloth painted with luminous stars.

'Your ticket?'

Phryne produced her ticket and the young man accepted it. He leaned close to her and whispered, 'Go in and take the chair by the door. Madame Stella is preparing for her trance and must not be disturbed. Please do not make a noise.'

Phryne was pushed through a curtain into a dim chamber dominated by a huge table set around with chairs. All but two were occupied. Phryne sat down and scanned her neighbours.

Sitting next to her was a fat woman in a flowered print and a chintz hat like a pot. She was over made-up and could not have acquired that colour of hair naturally. She smiled tremulously at Phryne and whispered, 'Isn't this exciting?'

A respectable widow occupied the next seat, then Maria Aliyena (alias Evans) and two men, both young, who were conferring together in low voices. They had a pencil and a block of paper before them, evidently to make notes. At the head of the table was the medium's cabinet, hung with thick black curtains. Next to it were two electric torches. Past the cabinet of mysteries were two men, in respectable clothes, who could have been clerks. From them floated a spiritual perfume, and Phryne thought that she could guess which bottle it came out of. Another man, middle-aged and greying, with a forgettable face and some difficulty in sitting, was next to them. Phryne was sure that this was her assailant. A foreign-looking girl with curly hair sat on Phryne's other side.

'You new here, dearie?' asked the fat woman.

'Yes, this is the first time. What do we do?' Phryne said.

'Wait until Madame Stella finishes her preparations, then we all hold hands and sing a hymn.'

'A hymn?'

'Yes, dear, it expels the evil spirits. Then we wait for Bright Feather to come through and he brings all the others.'

'Bright Feather?'

'Her control. He's a Red Indian. Shh!'

Madame Stella came in, escorted by a squat man in an academic robe. She was magnificent in long, dark draperies, with deep sleeves perfect for the concealment of apports. Phryne sat back and admired the atmosphere, cleverly created by having the customers wait in a darkened room with all these magical props and the luminous paint, which after a while began to induce light-spot illusions.

'God bless you,' began Madame Stella in her flat, common voice, and the congregation replied, 'God bless you.'

'All join hands and we will sing "Abide with Me."'

Phryne joined in, although this was not her favourite hymn. The anarchists appeared to have a political objection to carrying a tune.

> 'Abide with me, fast falls the eventide
> The darkness deepens, Lord with me abide,
> When other helpers fail, and comforts flee…
> In life, in death, O Lord, abide with me.'

Enough to scare every spirit right back to the Elysian Fields, she thought, easing the pressure of the foreign girl's fingers on her hand. Now. Let the play begin!

Madame Stella was leaning back in her chair, breathing deeply. Phryne counted the respirations; five, ten, fifteen, then a deep voice announced: 'Bright Feather is here. How!'

He sounded just like every Indian on every cowboy radio serial that Phryne had ever heard. She bit her lip so that she should not laugh, but the effect on the gathering was electric.

Phryne felt a shiver of excitement run through them. Someone gasped.

'Many spirits here,' commented Bright Feather. 'Tom wishes to speak to his mother. Is she here?'

The fat woman gave a sob of released tension and cried, 'Oh, Tom, are you all right?'

Phryne was suddenly very sorry for the fat woman. The medium stirred a little and produced another voice: a young man.

'Mother, I'm all right. It's nice here. Don't cry, Mother, don't mourn. You'll be with me soon.'

'Oh, Tommy,' the fat woman's voice faltered. 'Oh, my dear, my son! What's it like there, where you are?'

'All music and flowers, and Grandma is here. You remember Bill? He's here too. Lots of friends. Flowers…' The voice broke off. The fat woman clutched Phryne's hand and wept freely.

Bright Feather was back.

'An old man is calling for his wife. His hair is white. He is bent and walks with a stick. He says that his wife is called "Felicia." Is Felicia here?'

Phryne wondered why Bright Feather did not know who was waiting for this contact with the Other World.

The widow said dully, 'Is that you, Jack?'

'Hello, Lis, I got through at last.' The voice was creaky and disused. 'Lots of friends here. I brought you a present.'

Eerily, noiselessly, a speaking trumpet rose into the air, and moved slowly along to the widow. It tipped, and something rattled down onto the table.

'You lost it, didn't you, Lis? Always were careless,' creaked the old man's voice. The widow began to cry.

'Oh, Jack, it is you! I lost my wedding ring yesterday, I can't think where.'

Phryne had a shrewd idea where she had lost it. Here in the Socialist Bookshop, when she came to buy her ticket. Fraudulent mediums had to get their effects where they found them.

'What's it like, Jack? Beyond the veil? Do you miss me?'

'It's nice. We sing all day, flowers, music. No work to do.'

'Jack, Jack, did you meet Jesus?'

But Jack had gone. Something else was happening. A tambourine rose into the air and beat itself, jingling. The trumpet made a tootling noise. The curtains of the medium's booth billowed under the influence of a sudden wind.

Phryne was impressed. Madame Stella must have worked for hours to produce these effects.

A man came through for the two clerks, their old friend who had been killed by an omnibus driven by a drunk.

''Ello, 'ello, 'ello, who do we have here? You never used to believe in all this stuff, lads!'

'It's him!' exclaimed one of the clerks. 'Say something to him.'

Phryne was irresistibly reminded of *Hamlet*. 'It would be spoke to. Speak to it, Horatio!' The young man floundered.

'Are you all right, mate?'

'Of course. Nice here. You'll like it. Though I hope that driver burns in hell. He did for me, you know. Drunk as a Lord.'

'I thought you were supposed to leave all anger behind,' commented his friend, and Bright Feather took over again, cutting off the spirit's attempt to disabuse his friends about anger which lasted longer than life.

'He has much work to do before he can go on,' he said sternly. 'Many spirits cling to the passions of earth even though they are in the Happy Hunting Ground. I see the helpers coming to take him away. Now there is a young man. He passed on in a fire. He wants to speak to Casimir, Karl, Max, Nina and Maria. Are they here?'

'We are here,' said a solemn voice.

The medium's voice changed again. Phryne reflected that she must be getting tired. The advent of this anarchist was heralded by the most spectacular effect yet seen. Out of the dark, a fine cheese-cloth flag floated, red, with the hammer and sickle of the Revolution. Phryne caught a corner of it in her mouth as it floated down over the table, soundless, and sniffed.

The medium's saliva was rank upon it. Phryne spat it out.

The voice of this spirit was light. It was a young man's voice and he spoke entirely in Latvian. Phryne's attention wandered. She was still holding the hands of her neighbours. The fat woman sobbed gently. The foreign girl was listening hard.

One of the two young men took notes, the pencil scratching over the paper as he wrote down names and dates and, Phryne hoped, times and places. Occasionally the voice would say something which caused the Latvian-speaking part of the audience to gasp.

'What did he say?' Phryne whispered.

'He is talking about how he died,' the girl replied. 'He was in a siege. He says that he shot himself before the house burned down. We did not know that.'

And you still don't, thought Phryne. Bright Feather was back, and Phryne made ready to release her hands when an Irish voice said brightly, 'Well, me old dear! Do you remember the old Baker Fox Able?'

Chapter Nine

'Farewell, happy fields,
Where joy forever dwells! Hail, horrors! Hail!'

John Milton, *Paradise Lost*

Phryne was frozen with shock. How could anyone have known about Baker Fox Able? It was the designation of the plane in which she had, as a girl of nineteen, flown to the Hebrides in the 'Flu Epidemic, taking Dr. MacMillan to the stricken crofts. Irish Michael had been the only man at the airfield when she had borrowed the plane. The voice was Michael's voice, but he had been gone since 1921, when he had died in a flying accident.

'What is your name?' she faltered.

'Why, Michael, me darlin', Irish Michael as ever was. Nice to see you again, m'girl. You're doing well.'

'How did you die?'

'My plane fell out of the air, the wings just ripped off her and down she went. But it's all right being dead, *macushla*, don't you be afraid of it. I should have passed on years ago, but I'm still too interested in the earth…'

'Oh, Michael,' said Phryne, at a loss for something to say.

'So don't you worry, *mo chroidhe*. Lots of fliers here. Keep your chin up,' and he was gone.

The medium was stirring and opening her eyes. The lights were put on.

'Isn't that nice, someone came through for you.' The fat woman dried her eyes. 'Were you expecting him, dear?'

'No,' said a completely flabbergasted Phryne. 'No, I wasn't!'

Madame Stella gave Phryne a broad grin.

'It came through, didn't it? You knew him?'

'Yes, I knew him.'

'That's how it is with the bloody spirits, dearie. They always can surprise you. Good night,' she added. 'There's a cuppa downstairs if you want it, though if I was you I wouldn't touch the stuff. So long. I'm going to have a rest. The spirits take it out of you.'

Phryne found her way to the stairs, and at the bottom five anarchists were awaiting her.

'You are *la Chatte Noire?*'

'I am.' Phryne stared straight into the pale eyes of a young man. She pulled back the collar of the black dress and exhibited the tattoo. His eyes widened.

'I am Karl Smoller. This is Nina Gardstein. Maria Aliyena. Max Dubof. Casimir Svars.'

Casimir was the assailant with the crippled genitals. Karl Smoller was tall and blond; so was Max. They were of a height, and could easily have been the gunmen. She put their ages at about twenty-five.

'Come with us, so that we may discuss what is happening in Paris. We have not heard from the comrades for some time.'

'Neither have I. It is years since I was in Paris. I am not in contact with the comrades there.'

Phryne came further down the stairs, flexing her wrist to bring the throwing knife out of its sheath and into the palm of her right hand.

The women interested her. Maria with her fall of dead black hair, and the younger and prettier Nina, who had curly hair which was loosed to froth over her shoulders. It was red, growing out of a brown dye. She wondered why anyone would seek to conceal such beautiful hair. Nina had a heart-shaped face and pink cheeks. Around her neck a ring swung on a piece of string.

Nina would bear watching.

'Come with us,' repeated Karl. 'You have heard all of our plans, and must not be allowed to go free.'

'All your plans? I don't speak Latvian. I don't know what the spirits said. You have already attempted to kidnap me. Ask Casimir what happens to the man who lays a hand on me.'

'You are not a true anarchist,' snapped Casimir. 'No anarchist would harm a comrade.'

'Rubbish! You are attempting to harm me, all right.'

Stand-off. They backed away, allowing the other sitters to get to the tea. Phryne did not like either Max or Karl. Both of them had the pale-blue eyes which Bert said denoted a dangerous man. Phryne could not tell if she was making her point with them.

'We needed to speak with you.'

'You are speaking with me now.'

Phryne side-stepped until she had her back to the wall. Max and Karl confronted her. They were both taller and stronger than she was.

'You will come with us,' said Karl softly, allowing her to see the barrel of a pistol which was visible through his fingers. Phryne tossed up. This at least would take her where she wanted to go: to their stronghold. Presumably they had a car. Too dangerous, she decided.

'I will not come with you,' she said, closing her hand around the haft of the knife. 'And you will be sorry that you threatened me.'

The moment was perfectly poised. Phryne eyed her enemies. They looked competent and cold. She could not account for both of them before Karl could shoot.

'Nina, are you there?' A loud voice came from outside, the door shook under a heavy blow, and Nina Gardstein gasped with relief. She ran across in front of Karl and opened the door. A very large young man was about to knock again.

'Well, hello, how nice to see you!' exclaimed Phryne. 'I'm Phryne Fisher.'

She stepped forward, using Nina for cover, and took the large young man's arm.

'I am going to buy you both a drink,' she announced. 'Come along.'

Nina and her companion followed as Phryne emerged into the street. Looking back, she saw Karl put the gun back in his pocket and grinned into his scowling face.

'Another time, comrade.' Then she asked the newcomer, 'Who are you?'

The man, unexpectedly quick on the uptake, said easily, 'Bill Cooper. I'm a cane cutter. Come down to Melbourne when the season's over. How about that drink? And what were the commos going to do to you, eh?'

'I don't know, but I would not have enjoyed it. You walked in at exactly the right time. How long have you known Nina?'

'I met him three months ago, and we are going to be married,' announced Nina, exhibiting the ring strung around her neck. 'I am going to live in Queensland where they will never find me.'

'How can you stay with them? Aren't you afraid?'

'Me? Afraid? Of them?' snapped Nina. 'No! What can they do to me?'

'They could kill you and fling the body into the river,' said Phryne, grimly. 'You have flouted them and by your agency I have got away.'

'I keep telling her that,' said the cane cutter. 'But she won't listen.'

'I'll just find my taxi, it should be around here…ah, Bert, hello, Cec. Take us to a civilized pub.'

'You all right, Miss?'

'I nearly wasn't. This nice man rescued me. His name is Bill Cooper, and this is Nina Gardstein.'

Bert put the taxi at Spencer Street as one would put a horse at a fence.

'The Esplanade, Miss?'

'Yes, what a good idea.'

Phryne lit a cigarette. That had been a close shave.

Over a beer (Bill), a gin and tonic (Phryne) and a large
straight brandy (Nina), Phryne scanned her companions. Nina
was pretty, and when the dye was out of that red hair she would
be prettier. Although she wore the accepted revolutionary female
garb, she was curved in all the right places and would make a
toothsome armful indeed. Compared with Maria's fine-boned
wire-thin intensity, Nina was plump and vulgar, but she had
charm and a strong, sensual presence.

Bill Cooper the cane cutter was huge. He must have stood
over six feet tall and was several axe handles across the shoulders.
He had mild brown eyes like a cow and a closely cropped head of
brown hair, bleached in some places by the sun. He was burned
the colour of mahogany. His hands were as big as shovels. In his
city clothes he appeared bigger than life and his suit, bought
off-the-peg in some back-blocks general store, fitted only where
it touched and stretched dangerously across his mighty thighs
and his shoulders. Phryne summed him up as a lamb.

'So you want to go back to the comrades, Nina?'

'I have given my word, Bill. As soon as the action which is
in hand is finished, then I shall go with you to Queensland and
we shall be married and have many children.'

'How old are you, Nina?' Phryne asked.

'I am seventeen,' announced Nina, knocking back the brandy.
'I was born in Australia, my mother was a comrade. She died
three years ago—it was sad.'

'Why aren't you afraid? These are ruthless people.'

'Ruthless, yes, but they will not harm me. They are afraid
of my father.'

'Who is your father?'

Nina shook her head and held out her glass. Bill Cooper put
a big hand over the top of it.

'Tha's enough, m'girl. You'll spoil your complexion. You see
how it is, Miss Fisher. I come down to Melbourne last year and
I went to a pub in Spencer Street and she was there. I knew
right away that this was the girl for me. At first she pretended
not to speak English, but I kept coming back until she talked

to me and then we agreed to get married. She will come with me, to where there ain't no anarchists. But they are bad men, Miss Fisher, bad men. I've met some strange chaps on the fields. These are bad. They have guns. And what use will it be to say you'll marry me if you're in prison?'

'Will you wait for me, Bill?' Nina leaned on his shoulder. The cane cutter smiled and his rough face softened. The end of his broken nose wiggled.

'Of course I'll wait for you, love.'

'Nina, I must speak with you. Pay attention, love birds, and we may be able to get out of this with a whole skin. Tell me what was decided in the seance. Who came through?'

'George Gardstein and Peter Piatkov, who is called Peter the Painter.'

'George is some relation of yours?'

Nina chuckled, and took a sip of Bill's beer.

'He is dead,' she said dismissively. 'He died in the Siege of Sidney Street. He said that he was shot. This we did not know. It was thought that he died of burning.'

'Do you believe in the spirits?'

'Me? No. I know that these voices are not the spirits.'

'How do you know?'

Nina shook her head again and laughed. Phryne persisted.

'Well, what was decided? What did Gardstein say?'

'It is a secret.'

'I know that. Do you want to help me or not? Peter Smith is a friend of mine, you know. He is helping me.'

Nina froze with Bill's beer glass in her hand.

'You know Peter?'

'I do.' Phryne suppressed the information of how very well she knew him. 'He is my friend.'

'In that case I shall help you,' decided Nina. Bill hugged her.

'Good girl. You tell the lady what she wants to know. What is your interest, Miss?'

'I was driving past the Victoria Dock when my windscreen was shot out. I found a young man dying on the wharf approach road. I was shot at. I want those who killed the young man.'

'Poor Yourka. Maria is distraught. He was her cousin. He was a nice boy and the same age as me. All he did was to get drunk and boast. All young men get drunk and boast. It is part of being a young man. And they killed him.'

'They shot at you, Miss?'

Bill Cooper was shocked, and called for another beer. Nina had absent-mindedly drunk his.

'Yes. Here is my card. I am a private investigator. So I decided that since there are few enough beautiful young men in the world, and I had been shocked and my car damaged, I would find the murderers. I don't want anyone else. Nina and Maria are safe with me. But Karl and Max have got to go.'

'Mongrels,' commented Bill Cooper. 'You reckon you can get Nina out of all this without trouble with the cops, Miss?'

'I reckon,' agreed Phryne. 'If she will help me.'

Bill Cooper looked at Nina. He was waiting for her response. Phryne thought of Sir Gawain giving the Loathly Damsel her choice.

'I help you, of course.' Nina gulped down Bill's beer.

'Good. What did the medium say?'

'She say that the raid on the bank is to go ahead. She say that Thursday at two in the afternoon is the time. And that they should use the…the…'

'Lewis gun,' prompted Phryne, who had heard this English phrase dropped into the conversation with the spirits. Nina nodded.

'It was Peter Piatkov—*le Pierrot l'Peint'e*—who was supposed to be speaking. He says that he died in the Siege of Sidney Street. It is all lies.'

'All lies, is it? How do you know?'

'The medium, she is a fraud. Only sometimes do real spirits come through. Mostly it is all lies.'

'And you know that it is all lies,' reasoned Phryne, 'because you know that Peter Piatkov, Peter the Painter, did not die in Sidney Street...Oh, no, it's not that.' A light had burst on Phryne. 'You know that it is all lies because Peter the Painter isn't a spirit. You know that it is fraud because you know that Peter the Painter is alive!'

Nina gaped. Then she shook her head violently and shut her mouth as though her tongue had betrayed her.

'I won't tell anyone,' promised Phryne. 'Thursday of this week?' Nina nodded.

'Where?'

'State Savings Bank of Victoria, corner of William Street and Collins Street,' whispered Nina. 'If they know about Peter the Painter, they will kill me.'

'I heard it somewhere else, anyway,' soothed Phryne. 'Now. I expect that I will see you again. If you must go into that den of wolves, Nina, do be careful. I don't want another death on my conscience. Now I've got to go.'

'What's your hurry, Miss?' asked the cane cutter, affable with relief. 'Sit down and have another drink.'

'Can't. If I hurry I might catch the end of the ballet. 'Bye.' Phryne left the pub, collecting Bert and Cec on the way, and was driven to the Princess Theatre.

◇◇◇

'Ah, *le rideau*,' she said, as the drop curtain depicting a self-satisfied magician reclining on clouds was lowered. 'How has it been, ladies? Are you enjoying it?'

'Phryne,' observed Dr. MacMillan. 'The dancers are excellent. Really, the elevation is remarkable for human muscles. It's not that they leap so high, but seem to come down so slow.'

'Oh, so pretty,' sighed Jane. 'Lovely!'

Phryne collared a chocolate from the box resting on Ruth's lap. Dr. MacMillan was right. Nijinsky's slow vault was famous. Petroushka quivered and screamed against his imprisonment. Gypsies danced. A bear lumbered across the stage. Snow began to fall. High on a roof, the spirit of the murdered puppet shrieked and writhed in anguished protest against ever having been brought straw-limbed and with human heart into a ruthless world.

Phryne watched the magician trail his dead puppet across the crowded stage and reflected that the symbolism was a trace obvious.

The girls and Dr. MacMillan, caught up in the story, were on the verge of tears. Even Dot was sobbing.

'Poor Petroushka!' exclaimed Ruth, indignantly. Jane sniffed, and Dr. MacMillan supplied her with a huge handkerchief.

'Another curtain,' Phryne remarked. 'They are getting a full reception. Come on, ladies. Bert and Cec are waiting.'

'Poor Petroushka,' echoed Jane, as she followed Phryne out of the box and onto the grand staircase. 'It wasn't fair!'

Phryne, thinking of Yourka and Nina, agreed that it was not fair. The emotions of both the girls were mollified by time and the purchase of a hand-painted programme.

Phryne put herself to bed in her own house in possession of more dangerous information than she felt that she could handle.

◇◇◇

And where was Alicia Waddington-Forsythe?

Chapter Ten

'Secrets with girls, like loaded guns with boys,
Are never valued till they make a noise.'
George Crabbe, *Tales of the Hall*

The morning dawned with the furious ringing of the telephone. It woke Phryne, who had slept lightly, worrying about bank robberies and missing girls. It brought Mr. Butler out of his own quarters with a piece of buttered toast in his hand.

'Miss Fisher's residence,' he articulated, spattering crumbs. 'No, madam, Miss Mary is not here.'

At that moment the door bell rang. Mr. Butler said into the phone, 'If you will excuse me, madam, just one moment…'

Phryne, at the head of the stairs, heard the door open.

Mr. Butler allowed someone to enter, then resumed his conversation.

'Mrs. Tachell? Miss Mary has just arrived. I gather that she has come to see Miss Fisher. No, madam, she is quite well. Yes, madam, I will ask Miss Fisher to call you as soon as she is in possession of the facts. Certainly, madam. A pleasure, madam. Good morning.'

Mr. Butler broke the connection. Phryne flowed down the stairs in her silver-and-jade lounging robe and silver slippers in time to receive a hysterical girl who flung herself into Phryne's silk-clad embrace.

'Oh, Miss Fisher, I had to come!' sobbed Mary Tachell.

Phryne, who had little patience for being cried over, hugged the girl tight and drew her into the salon.

'Ask Mrs. Butler for some breakfast, Mr. B., or at least some tea. Is Dot up yet? And the girls, if you please. We seem to have come to some crux.'

'Not the girls…' wept Mary, and Phryne sat her down in a big chair and handed her a handkerchief.

'Now, now, Mary, don't take on so,' she chided. 'No need for all this emotion so early in the morning.'

Mr. Butler reclaimed his piece of toast and retreated to the kitchen, where Mrs. Butler, Dot, Jane and Ruth were breakfasting.

'Your schoolfellow has arrived,' he announced to the girls, 'in a tizz. Miss Fisher wants tea.'

Dot poured boiling water into the company teapot and assembled cups and cutlery. Jane bolted her porridge.

'No hurry, Jane,' said Dot. 'Miss Phryne don't like being interrupted when she's talking to someone. Give it ten minutes,' and Dot sailed into the salon with the tray, unloaded it, and came back to report that Mary Tachell was still weeping freely and would go on doing so for some time.

'Gosh,' said Ruth, buttering another piece of toast and lavishing Oxford marmalade on it. 'I wonder what's happened?'

'I bet,' replied Jane, 'that she has read Alicia's diary.' Mary Tachell stopped crying to drink her tea and sniff at the sal volatile which Dot had thoughtfully provided. The child was distraught. Her pale eyes were as red as lillipilli berries and her complexion blotched into a parody of her *Alice in Wonderland* self. Phryne noticed that through all that emotional collapse she had kept tight hold of a book, bound in purple leather, with *Firenze* embossed on the cover.

'I went to the Domain Gardens this morning,' sobbed Mary. 'I found the diary. I caught the tram to take me here, and on the way I…I…'

'Read the diary,' prompted Phryne, who would not have been able to resist reading it under the circumstances. 'Never mind.'

'Oh, Miss Fisher, it's what was in the diary! Alicia, she…she…'

'Don't take on so, Mary. If you can't tell me, then give me the book. It can't be that bad.'

'Oh, it is!' and poor Mary wept again. Phryne summoned Ruth and Jane from the kitchen door, where she had spotted them lurking, and they came forward to embrace Mary Tachell, sitting either side of her in the big chair. Mary turned her face into Jane's flat adolescent chest.

'Never mind, Mary,' soothed Ruth. 'You've done the right thing, bringing the diary to Miss Fisher. She'll find Alicia.'

'I don't…I don't know whether I want her to find Alicia after what I read in her diary,' confessed Mary. 'And she's my only friend!'

Mary howled and Jane patted her helplessly.

'We'll be your friends, won't we, Ruth?' Ruth muttered something about ninnies, and then said aloud, 'Of course we will.'

'Will you let me join your club?' demanded Mary, from the depths of her disordered hair. Jane sighed.

'Yes, I suppose so. Stop crying, now.'

'Take her into the kitchen, girls, and give her some breakfast,' said Phryne, leafing through the diary. 'I'll be with you directly.'

Ruth and Jane took Mary away.

'Let's see, now. What beautiful handwriting the child has. Convent educated, obviously. Have a look, Dot.'

'Yes, Miss, nice convent hand. I used to write like that, when I was at school.'

'What do these mean? Prime, matins, nones?'

'They're the conventual hours, Miss. The nuns go to church at set times during the day and the night.'

'Really? When do the poor things sleep?'

'Between midnight and dawn, Miss. See—she says that she wants to be a nun.'

'"I think I have a vocation, and Reverend Mother thinks so too,"' read Phryne. '"It is my destiny to be a nun. I wish I was a Catholic! It is easier for them. Their family would think it was an honour. But Father won't allow it, he got into a frightful state when I tried to talk to him. Mem: remember the tortures of the martyrs. I wish I could torture Father. It's not as if he wants me. He is in love with Christine. So is Paul. She is the Scarlet Woman. I wish she would die."

'Strong words, Dot.'

'Yes, Miss, but you can see why she feels like that. And it's true about Catholic families. My mum wanted me to become a nun. When I was twelve I thought that I had a vocation, too. Lots of little Catholic girls want to be nuns. Poor little thing, they should have left her in the convent. She might have grown out of it.'

'I'll skim through this bit…complaints about her father… rude comments about Christine…aha!

"'I could not sleep and I am keeping the Hours. Last night I saw Paul coming out of Christine's room, when Father was at the lodge meeting. She kissed him at the door. She kissed him like a lover. It's awful!!! What shall I do? My father is dishonoured. I shall have to tell him!'"

'It is as the girls thought, Miss,' said Dot soberly. 'I wonder what she did?'

'Not much more, Dot. Bear up. And he is the most beautiful young man. Pregnant women have their fancies.'

'Miss, how pregnant is Mrs. Waddington-Forsythe?'

Phryne stared at Dot, looked at the date of the diary entry, and whistled.

'For a well brought-up girl, Dorothy, you have the most indecent imagination. And you are quite right. I put Mrs. W. at about five months. This entry is six months old. And I thought that the old goat was overpleased at having sired a child. Oh, Lord, Dot, what can have happened to Alicia? Dynamite stuff! Did she speak to her father?'

'Go on with the diary, Miss.'

There were ten pages left. On one was written the address of a famous alienist who practised in Collins Street, and a time.

'I presume that this was an appointment,' commented Phryne. 'We must speak to Dr. Honeycombe. What more from Alicia, then?

'"Paul has been unfaithful to me,"' read Phryne disbelievingly. '"He said that he'd never love anyone but me. Now he is in love with Christine. Just because she's older and has a better shape. Paul has loved me since I was twelve. He is mine. I was going to give him up to be a Bride of Christ but now Father says that I have to go to some school in the city. He wants me to make a good marriage. I am not fit for marriage. The man would know. I have been a great sinner,"' continued the diary, a shade complacently. '"Now that Father will not allow me to be a nun, the only thing I can do is die and let God judge me. Holy Mary Mother of God have mercy on all sinners!"'

'The man would know,' said Dot. 'What would he know?'

'That she wasn't a virgin, Dot,' said Phryne gently. 'Paul has been spreading himself about a bit, hasn't he?'

'Lord deliver us!'

'And I have a good idea what has happened to Alicia. Let's finish the diary. Do you feel all right, Dot?'

'No, but let's finish it, there can't be anything else.'

'"Christine wants me to see Dr. Honeycombe,"' concluded the diary. '"I am to go there tomorrow. Because I tried to run away. And I shall run away again. And if I'm dead they won't be able to find me then. Reverend Mother says that God ordains a vocation."'

'Get me Mrs. Waddington-Forsythe on the phone, Dot, and then find the Reverend Mother's number.'

Phryne's face was so stern that Dot, considerably shaken, did her bidding swiftly.

'Mrs. Waddington-Forsythe? Phryne Fisher. How are you? Good,' Dot heard Phryne purr. 'And your health? Excellent. Now I won't keep you on the telephone, I'm sure that you must be worried about Alicia. You are? I see. Now, pay attention, and don't make an outcry, because you will have to explain it. I know about Paul, the paternity of that cuckoo you are carrying, and what you did to Alicia. I hope that she is well, or I shall have to expose you. Give me the address of the clinic and then a written document, signed by your repulsive husband to the effect that

Alicia has his full permission to be a nun. When? Today. I shall go and fetch her immediately. Send it around by car within the hour. Mr. Waddington-Forsythe is at home, is he? Good. If Alicia is all right, then you will hear nothing more about this. If she is not, then I fear that I will have to reveal all.'

Some panicky protests could be heard. Phryne held the phone away from her ear, and then resumed it.

'Got that over with? Good. The address, please.'

Phryne scribbled on the writing paper which Mr. Butler had left on the table. He liked his telephone books to be neat.

'I've got that. And an order from you for her release, please. You will call the doctor directly, won't you? If I meet with any check in this rescue, I shall not be pleased.'

Gabbled reassurances reached Dot three feet away.

'I shall call you again when the matter is complete. Don't go out, will you? I may need your testimony. Good morning.' Phryne slammed down the phone, picked it up again, and asked for the Eltham number.

'Dot, ask Mr. B. for the car. Blankets and brandy. Hello, this is Phryne Fisher, can I speak to Reverend Mother? Yes, I'll hold the line. Dot, get that poor Mary cleaned up to go home and send her there in a taxi as soon as poss. Tell the girls that I can't take them to the beach this morning. Get Bert or Cec to go with them as bodyguard if they want to go out—and you, too. Be careful. We are still knee deep in anarchists. Hello? Yes, I'm waiting for Reverend Mother. It is urgent. Yes, I'll hold... tell Mr. B. we are going to Eltham and then to...aha. Good morning, Reverend Mother. Phryne Fisher.'

'Good morning, Miss Fisher.' The voice was cool and faintly amused, as always. Phryne could picture the magnificent study with the bow windows looking onto the garden full of plum blossom.

'I've found Alicia, and I want you to come and rescue her.'

'Where is she? I will come, of course. Is she...was it... Gertrude Street?'

'No, worse. She's in a private mental clinic on the Plenty Road, rather near your convent, actually.'

'And is she insane?'

'Well, she wasn't a few days ago, but what she might be now, who can tell? She has had the most frightful experience, which I will tell you about when I see you. Will you come, and will you accept her as a...novice? Is that the term? If she is still of sound mind?'

'But her father...'

'Her father has no further objections.'

'As long as the poor little thing has her own wits and wants to be a nun, Miss Fisher, then God would be very cross with me if I did not accept her.'

'I'm glad. I'll be with you as soon as I can.'

'Anything I can do in the meantime?'

'Pray,' advised Phryne. Reverend Mother chuckled.

'Good advice,' she agreed. 'I shall see you soon, Miss Fisher.'

Phryne called Bert and Cec at their boarding house.

'Bert? Can you come and look after the girls for me?'

'I ain't much good at baby sitting, Miss,' protested Bert.

'Yes, you are. I am under threat by the anarchists and I can't attend to it myself. I need some guards. I can't keep them inside all the time. Besides, I don't want them to think that they've frightened me. Are you on?'

'Yes, Miss,' agreed Cec, who had taken over the phone. 'You want us armed?'

'Yes,' said Phryne. She heard Cec draw a deep breath.

'You know what will happen to us if we are sprung carrying concealed firearms, don't you, Miss?'

'Yes.'

'All right, Miss, see you in a tick.'

Dot brushed past Phryne, with an armful of blankets and the brandy flask. Phryne picked up the phone again.

'Russell Street,' she ordered. 'Detective-Sergeant Carroll. Yes, I'll wait.'

'Miss? Mary Tachell wants to go home.'

'In a minute, Dot. Can you go outside and watch for a car from the Waddington-Forsythe pest house? It's bringing me two letters and I want to read them before it goes back. Find me a pencil that writes, will you? I've broken this one. And Bert and Cec are coming to look after you while I'm away. Hello? Bill? Phryne Fisher. I've got some news. The State Bank on the corner of William…yes, the big one…Thursday at two in the afternoon. And they've got a Lewis gun, so be careful…'

Phryne accepted a newly pointed pencil from Dot and immediately broke it on the writing paper. 'Listen, you great lump of a cop, I risked my life for this info, and I can't tell you where I got it, but the provenance is impeccable…straight from the horse's mouth, so to speak…'

'Don't get so excited, Miss Fisher,' said the calm voice. 'I believe you. It's them I don't believe. Them commos, the truth ain't in them, and they ain't got no sense of planning. But thank you for the office, Miss. I'll tell my boss. It'll be up to him what we do about it.'

'Well, don't say I didn't warn you,' said Phryne, and hung up. She ran upstairs and threw on an assortment of clothes.

'Coffee!' she called, walking into the kitchen, where Mrs. Butler had anticipated the request and was stirring Greek coffee, water, and sugar in a pan. Mary Tachell, mopped up and fed, was in the girls' room listening to their phonograph. Mr. Butler was finishing his breakfast wearing a chauffeur's cap, his greatcoat hung over the door.

'Thanks, Mrs. B. We'll all be out of your hair in a minute. I'm going to this address, Mr. Butler, can you look up the map? First we have to go back to the convent and get Reverend Mother. Better put in a blanket for her, too.'

'Travelling rugs are in the car, Miss, and the brandy you ordered. Here's your coffee, Miss. Have you found the little girl?' asked Mrs. Butler, hopefully.

'Yes, I have found her, but there are more problems. Mr. Bert and Mr. Cec are coming to take Mary Tachell home, then they will come back and look after the girls and you. Don't leave the house without a guard. And keep all the windows locked.'

'Good Lord, Miss, are you fighting a war?'

'A small war, and soon over,' soothed Phryne. 'I'll be back as soon as I can. I'm not taking Dot with me. Probably nothing will happen. And if you get a phone call ostensibly from me to go to the docks in the dark, alone, do me a favour and disregard it, won't you?'

Mrs. Butler promised.

The Waddington-Forsythe car arrived before Phryne had finished her coffee. Dot brought the letters into the house. Phryne broke the seals and read them.

'One to Reverend Mother stating that Alicia can profess religion if she wishes. Good. It's signed by Mr. W. And one to Dr. Honeycombe stating that Alicia is to be released into my custody, signed, by both father and stepmother. I wonder how she managed to get him to sign that? Has the whole thing been exposed? I bet it hasn't. Another letter; addressed to me. Well. Scribbled on the ripped-out page of an exercise book by someone using indelible pencil and in a terrible hurry. "Miss Fisher I never knew, I never knew what happened to Alicia. She never told me. Tell Alicia I'm sorry. I'm sorry. Paul." Hmm. Come on, Mr. B., we're on the road.'

Bert and Cec drew up as the long red Hispano-Suiza manoeuvred itself into the street. Phryne had time to yell a greeting before Mr. Butler, enjoined to drive like the wind, put his foot down and the racing engines whined with delight. Phryne leaned back to enjoy the rush of air past her face.

Plenty Road unwound before her as the big car ate the miles. Phryne attempted a little meditation, failed to keep her mind on the Coué, 'every day in every way I am getting better and better.' analysed her objection to it as pure bad temper, and smoked her way through half a packet of Virginia gaspers until the car turned into the convent drive. The house struck Phryne afresh. What effect would all those gargoyles have on a young woman in shaky possession of her wits? Reverend Mother's little helpers conducted her out of the house and into the big red car next to Phryne, whose black cloche with red hibiscus flowers attracted much whispering.

'Reverend Mother.'

'Miss Fisher.' The tall woman smiled politely. 'This is an adventure! Tell me all.'

Phryne handed her the purple-bound diary and said, 'Read the last three pages, if you please. Off we go, Mr. B. The Sunshine Nursing Home, and step on it.'

Mr. Butler eased the Hispano-Suiza out of the convent drive and Reverend Mother leafed through the book.

'Lord, Miss Fisher, the poor girl. What a history! No wonder her reason collapsed under it.'

'Her reason didn't collapse.' Phryne was terse. 'She was put away. Her stepmamma knew that no one would believe her. Her reason might have collapsed by now, of course, nothing like a few days of people telling you that you are mad and deluded when you know that you are telling the truth to turn the brain.'

'Is this Dr. Honeycombe an…accomplice, then?'

'Don't know. Will you still accept her, now that you know her history?'

'Accept her? Of course. She's only a child. Her brother has abused her. Poor little thing.'

Mr. Butler stopped outside a large country house. It was an old farm house, with verandahs all around, and only the construction of a tall brick wall and the insertion of an imposing iron gate with a guard made it any different from its neighbours.

'Miss Fisher to see Dr. Honeycombe,' snapped Mr. Butler to the uniformed guard. Mr. Butler did not like loony-bins. The guard allowed the car to pass and latched the gate behind it.

'I don't like being locked in,' commented Phryne. 'To the house, please, Mr. B.'

Mr. Butler stopped the car, and doubled around to assist Miss Fisher and the nun. Phryne stalked up the steps onto the verandah, to be confronted by a large man clad in a hospital gown. He made a monkey noise, bounced a couple of times, and turned to reveal that his buttocks had been painted red, white and blue. Phryne presumed that the choice of colours was patriotic.

'Very nice,' she said into his gibbering face as he whisked around. 'Let me pass.'

Reverend Mother was leaning on the verandah rail, white to the veils. Phryne plucked at her arm.

'It's only a man,' she said. 'Come along.'

At that moment the door banged open and a pair of very big men in white coats hurtled out, seized the ape man, and hauled him whimpering away.

'What a *nice* place. Hello! Anyone there?'

A flustered nurse emerged and escorted them inside.

'Oh, dear, ladies, I am sorry. He gets away, you know, and he's that strong I couldn't hold him! Who did you want to see, Miss?'

'I've got a letter for the custody of Alicia Waddington-Forsythe,' said Phryne, supporting Reverend Mother. 'Take me to her, if you please.'

'I'll do that, Miss, but you shall have to sign her out. Dr. Honeycombe will want to see you, Miss.'

'I should like to see him, too. Now, Alicia Waddington-Forsythe, if you please, and look slippy about it!'

The nurse smoothed back her hair and led the way down a seagrass corridor to a small room.

'She's locked in, Miss, and she ain't got no clothes, because she tried to kill herself.'

'Mr. Butler, go back to the car and fetch a rug, please. Now, nurse, unlock that door and then bring me Dr. Honeycombe.'

The nurse unlocked the door. Phryne opened it. Sitting in the exact middle of the bare floor was Alicia Waddington-Forsythe. She was naked and her hair was tangled; she had scratches along her throat and a dark red ring around it. Reverend Mother stopped Phryne and said, 'Listen.'

Drearily, hopelessly, Alicia Waddington-Forsythe was praying.

'She'll be all right,' said the Reverend Mother, sweeping into the cell. She knelt down beside Alicia and they completed the prayer together.

'*Ave Maria, pleni gratia…*'

Phryne was joined at the door by a dapper man with a Freudian beard, exuding the scent of expensive cologne. He clicked his tongue disapprovingly.

'Religion! The girl has an Oedipal mania and they give her religion!'

'Dr. Honeycombe, I presume. Read this, if you please.'

'Are you Miss Fisher? But we are making progress with this patient. She has stopped denying her delusions. Another few days and she would be admitting that they are all fantasies. A well-marked complex. She believes that her brother and she were lovers, and that her brother has transferred his affections to her stepmother, of whom she is jealous.'

'Oh? What treatment have you been giving her?'

'The usual. Consultation, a low diet, and firmness. The patient must understand that her delusions are…well…delusory.'

'And how have you been going with getting her to admit that they aren't true?'

'Well, I think, very well. After the first day she stopped asserting that they were true. We have not yet brought her to the point of healthily admitting that they are not true, and last night she tried self-destruction. You can see the marks. She tried to hang herself, so we have removed all cloth that could be used to make ropes. In another few days, perhaps weeks, she would have come to the realization that her family is like all other families and then she could have gone home.'

'Tell me, Dr. Honeycombe, how does it feel to be a cretin?' Dr. Honeycombe stepped back from Phryne's furious face.

'I beg your pardon?'

'It's all true, Doctor. Her family is not like any other. She was sleeping with her brother and he did transfer his attentions to her stepmother and the stepmother is presently pregnant with the brother's child, and you made her deny it.'

'She did not deny,' admitted Dr. Honeycombe. 'Are you sure?' He was examining Phryne as if he wondered whether she was involved in a *folie à deux* with Alicia.

'I am sure. And I am taking her away. Now. Get out of my way.' Mr. Butler gave the rug to Reverend Mother, who wrapped Alicia in it. Dr. Honeycombe stepped back. Mr. Butler lifted Alicia and carried her down the corridor and out of the Sunshine Nursing Home and laid her in Reverend Mother's lap in the back of the car. Phryne paused to sign the register with such vengeful force that she destroyed the nib, then ran down and jumped in.

'Off we go, Mr. Butler, and if they close the gate just drive through it!'

The gate was open. Mr. Butler considered this fortunate.

'Phew! What a place. How is Alicia?'

'She has been doped, I think. I told her that I knew all about her history, and I was sure that God would forgive her. She said she still wants to be a nun.'

Phryne got her first look at Alicia in the flesh. A strong face, stubborn, determined. They had been able to make her stop asserting the truth, but they had not managed to make her deny it. She had tried to die rather than agree that she had told lies. This was the metal of which martyrs were forged. She was clutching Reverend Mother's hand and her pectoral cross with similar fervour.

'Do you want to be a nun, Alicia? You don't have to go back to your revolting family.' Phryne was firm. She needed an answer before she allowed the child to be delivered to another custodian. Alicia opened her eyes. Phryne gave her a sip of brandy.

'I can be a nun?' asked a voice weakened by screaming. 'Even though…there was Paul? Even though…Christine…'

'Even though,' agreed Reverend Mother. 'You can make your own choice. No one is pressing you, Alicia.'

'In any case,' she added to Phryne, 'she cannot take her final vows for years yet. She can stay with us and she can leave, as well. Anglican sisters are not enclosed, you know, Miss Fisher.'

'I want to be a nun.' Alicia's eyes became moist. 'God has called me. He said that you would come, Reverend Mother. I knew you would come.'

'All right, a nun you shall be. Here we are at the convent. Can you find my Mr. Butler a drink and a bite, Mother? And I would not say no to a bit of a sit down myself. It has been a busy morning.'

'Yes, it is almost time for lunch. If your driver would carry Alicia again, we must get her to bed, and I shall call the convent doctor to have a look at her throat.'

'No doctors!' wailed Alicia, and the tall woman patted her.

'I shall be there the whole time. Now, you are in no danger. No one can take you away from us. You are part of this religious community from now on and you are under obedience, Alicia.' Alicia smiled.

Phryne accepted a cooling lemon drink (which would have been improved by the addition of ice and gin, she considered) after she had seen Alicia put to bed in the infirmary with a rosary to occupy her mind and the infirmarian, a plump and jolly nun, within call.

'I think that she will do very well,' remarked Reverend Mother. 'She has firmness of mind. Will there be any trouble with her family? Her father, perhaps, who presumably does not know of all this, will he want her back?'

'No. I don't know what tale the adorable Christine has told him to get him to sign that custody agreement, but it won't have been the true one. It means that Alicia is more-or-less an orphan, though. Have a look at this.'

'The brother, Paul, he wrote this? Interesting. It appears that he did not know what had happened to Alicia. I suppose that even in such a criminal affection there may be some dregs of a real regard. May I keep this? I shall show it to Alicia—perhaps— when it seems expedient.'

'By all means. If you receive any communications from that family, and I mean anything, please call me. You know my telephone number. If the poor girl has a chance of being happy, I do not want Papa to louse it up.'

Wincing somewhat at the slang, Reverend Mother nodded.

'That lemon drink is a little insipid, isn't it?' she asked, reaching into her desk drawer. 'A nip of gin may improve it. After all, it is not every day that the prodigal returns.'

Phryne held out her glass.

'Bottoms up,' she said, and Reverend Mother laughed.

Chapter Eleven

'...and I
Play too, but so disgraced a part, whose issue
Will hiss me to my grave.'
William Shakespeare, *The Winter's Tale*

Cec tightened his belt around the British Bulldog .45 which he had brought home from Gallipoli (the present of an English officer, whom he and Bert had rescued from a collapsing trench) and said casually, 'Reckon that the beach should be the safest, eh, mate?'

Bert surveyed the terrain with the eyes of the gunner he once had been. Undulating dunes, too low for cover, and a good view along the shore for half a mile.

'Reckon,' he agreed. 'Come on, girls.'

Bert and Cec, although inexperienced at babysitting, were familiar with the role of guard. They crossed the road carefully, tiptoeing across the sand and scrub, Bert leading, Cec taking rearguard.

'Do you really think we'll be attacked?' asked Ruth, breathlessly. She had a taste for adventure which her friend and adoptive sister did not share. Jane would have been content to stay at home behind an adequate number of locked doors.

'Dunno,' grunted Bert. 'But Miss thinks that you might. No sense in taking chances with them anarchists. Here we are. No one on the beach and a nice day for swimming.'

'Are you coming in, too?' asked Jane, nervously. Bert grinned.

'Not today. Too early in the year for me. I'll just sit here and watch yer.'

Jane and Ruth disrobed, revealing decorous red and yellow costumes with backs and legs, and pulled on rubber bathing caps. They raced each other down to the shore and plunged in, squealing at the cold touch of the water.

'You all right to see that way, mate?'

Behind him, Cec said, 'Reckon,' and Bert rolled a cigarette.

'Beg pardon, Miss, do you mind?' he asked Dot, who was sitting next to him on the sand and watching the swimmers.

'Go ahead,' said Dot. 'I wonder if Miss Phryne's got that Alicia back?'

'She's gone off to do that, has she? If the girl is there, you can bet Miss'll get her. Very determined sheila, Miss Phryne is. Sing out when you want a smoke, Cec.'

'All right, mate.'

The sun was warm, without the sting of summer, and Dot was sleepy. The girls called like birds in the embrace of the sea. Dot closed her eyes.

An hour later, Jane and Ruth were chilled and exhilarated and were racing each other up the sand when there was a noise like a motorcar backfire. A spurt of sand was kicked up.

'Get down!' roared Bert, and both girls dropped to the ground.

'They're shooting at us!' exclaimed Ruth, indignantly.

'Stay still!' wailed Jane. 'Oh, Lord, I wish I'd never come swimming.'

Cec sighted the gunman. He was standing in the scrub, wearing a grey hat. Cec caught sight of a pistol and knew that it did not have sufficient range to do any great harm.

'He's in the scrub, Bert, ten degrees west. Got a pistol.'

'I'll go back to the house,' gasped Dot, and ran forward, eluding Bert's grab at her arm.

'No, Miss, don't move…he hasn't got the range without moving…he wants to flush us out. Dot!' bellowed Bert, but Dot kept running.

'What'll we do, mate?' asked Cec. 'If we follow her we'll leave the girls unguarded.'

'You stay here and keep that sniper pinned down,' decided Bert. 'I'll go after Dot, she's lost her head.' He drew his pistol and moved across the sand in the sideways scuttle learned on many excursions over the top.

Bert reached the road unscathed, just in time to see Dot being dragged into a black car. He yelled, and as the car gunned the engine and roared past him, fired a couple of shots at the tyres.

He knew that he had hit something as the car swerved, but the driver recovered and vanished. Bert swore, trousered his gun, and found a stub of pencil which he licked, then used to write down the car's number on his far-from-white cuff.

The pistol shooter had stopped. Cec was beckoning from the bushes.

'Look at this, mate,' exclaimed Cec. 'We've been set up.' He reeled in yards of green fishing line.

'Simple,' snorted Bert. 'Jam an automatic into this bush and pull the trigger with a bit of cutty hunk. Knew we couldn't see good through these bloody branches. All they got to do is wait on the road.'

'Where's Dot?' wailed Jane.

'They got her,' said Bert. 'We're going back to the house. What Miss Phryne's gonna say to us I don't like to think.'

Bert took the grey hat which perched insolently on a twig and threw it to the ground, stamping on it.

◇◇◇

Dot sat huddled in the corner of the big car, swathed in a blanket which she gathered must have been used to wrap engine parts from the way it smelt, and shivered. She had not seen her attackers. She had skidded across the sand for the house even though Bert had told her not to move, and now she was caught like a rabbit in a trap. She was ashamed of herself, terrified of what Phryne would say, and horrified about what had happened on the beach. Were the others all right? Had they all been shot?

This left very little attention to be spared for worrying about herself. She strained her ears, but her captors were speaking in a foreign language. She was in the hands of foreigners!

Gradually, as she got used to not being able to see, her hearing sharpened and she began to pick out words. Then she allowed herself a small giggle.

They thought that they had Phryne Fisher.

What would they do when they found out that they were wrong?

Dot told herself sternly not to cry, but after the third rough turn which bruised her against unseen obstacles, she wept.

◇◇◇

Phryne had an agreeable lunch with the Reverend Mother, bade Alicia farewell in the middle of the 'Third Sorrowful Mystery,' and preened herself all the way home on how well the adventure had gone. She tripped lightly up her steps and burst into the hall singing a little song about the flowers that bloom in the spring but the tra-la died on her lips.

Jane and Ruth were sitting on the sofa wearing bathing suits and weeping into each other's hair. Cec and Bert were standing glumly in the hall, staring into space, like soldiers awaiting a court martial.

'What has happened?' asked Phryne. 'Bert?'

'We were attacked,' began Bert. 'And…they got Dot.'

'What, hurt? Not dead?' cried Phryne, supporting herself on the doorpost.

'No, Miss, as far as we know she's all right, but they snatched her. A big black car—Bentley. Here's the number.' Bert exhibited his shirt cuff.

'Anarchists?' asked Phryne grimly. 'Of course. Tell me all about it, and how they managed to get around two such experienced diggers.'

Bert and Cec, interrupting each other, explained.

'A trap! And a very good trap, too. Right. Everyone stop crying. I don't blame you, Bert, Cec. They won't have hurt her. They either think they have me, or they want someone to ensure that I do not interfere with their plots. We must find out where they are. Get out there and pull a few strings. Call in some favours. I want to know where their hide-out is. Get cracking. Ruth, Jane, do stop crying, you aren't hurt. We will get Dot back. Pull yourselves together. I might need you. Oh, and your friend Alicia is all right. She's back at the convent and will stay there. Now go and wash your faces, do. And put some clothes on. Mr. Butler!'

He appeared at her elbow.

'Yes, Miss Fisher?'

'Lock everything. No visitors. Though I doubt that they'd try again. It depends. We shall not risk it. Mrs. Butler, give the girls some lunch, will you? I've eaten. I have to think, so I'm going to my room and I don't want to be disturbed unless it's urgent.'

Phryne ran up the stairs, shut herself into her rooms, and threw herself into her padded chair. What to do?

After ten minutes' hard cogitation she was forced to the conclusion that all she could do was wait.

Then she had a sudden inspiration, and rang Constable Collins to tell him that Dot would not be going to the Latvian Club with him that night.

The young man sounded resigned.

'She's changed her mind, Miss?'

'No, she's been kidnapped. Can you find a car registration for me?'

'She's been *what*?'

'Kidnapped, aren't you listening? The anarchists took her this morning. Can you find a car number for me?'

'Miss, have you reported this to the police?'

'No. I want her back alive, and I don't want a lot of heavy-footed cops blundering around and getting her killed. For the third time, can you...'

'Yes, Miss, what's the number?'

Phryne read it out. The young voice said worriedly, 'Can't I help, Miss? I really like Miss Williams. I...I think she likes me.'

'So do I. All right, but in a private capacity, and if you get caught then say farewell to the police force.'

'I don't mind, Miss.'

'Good, then find me that address and ring back. I'll use you, if I think that you can help.'

'Deal,' said Constable Collins promptly, and hung up. It was a trying afternoon. No one called. Peter Smith came to dinner. Phryne was in no mood for men, or even for food. There was still no word from the kidnappers.

However, here they both were, and Phryne was a social animal.

Mrs. Butler had provided French onion soup with black bread bought from the German bakery in Acland Street. There was a roast of veal with new potatoes and green salad to follow, and cheese and fruit for dessert. Peter Smith was still amiable and intelligent and might be in collusion with the anarchists, so had to be mollified. Phryne considered that she had made a good fist of it throughout dinner and she was about to propose that they adjourn to her boudoir when the phone rang.

'Constable Collins, Miss. The address of that car is 168A Fitzroy Street, St. Kilda. Have you had any word?'

'No. Call here after you have been to the Latvian Club, eh? I might know more by then. 'Bye.'

'Peter, I need your help,' she said as she came back into the salon. 'Come upstairs with me.

'Now, grab hold of this whisky and look me in the eye. Did you know that your anarchist mates have kidnapped my maid?'

Peter Smith did not flinch. 'I did not know.'

'Did you know that they are intending to rob the State Bank in the city on Thursday at two o'clock?'

'I did not know.'

'Do you know who lives at 168A Fitzroy Street, St. Kilda?'

'Nina and Maria live there.'

'The others?'

'Smith Street, Collingwood. I can show you the house.'

'Will you?'

'Yes.'

'Why are you helping me?'

'Because I love you. And because they have betrayed the Revolution, for which I would have died. They want to ruin Australia, as they have ruined America. There is no free thinking in the USA, now, thanks to anarchist outrages. Fools. Have you had word?'

'Nothing.'

Peter reflected, sipping the whisky.

'I wonder if they wanted you and have taken the wrong woman?'

'What then?'

'They may kill her. It depends on whether she has seen them.'

'If they kill Dot, then they all die,' said Phryne, with icy calm. 'Why should they kill her?'

'Because she is not you. But I do not expect that they will even hurt her. Where did you find out about the date and time of the robbery?'

'From the medium, Jean Vassileva.'

'Ah, Madame Stella—surely they don't still believe in all that spiritualist nonsense?'

'Most of it was nonsense,' agreed Phryne. 'But some of it was sense. I heard from an old friend, who produced the number of a plane I once flew.'

'I'm not saying that the spirits don't exist, Phryne, just that Madame Stella has only a passing acquaintance with them. So, they told you tomorrow at two, eh?'

'Yes, that's what Nina said. The conversation was in Latvian.'

'I wonder if that's exactly what Madame Stella said.'

'What does it matter?'

'Ah, you are not a revolutionary, madam. Add one day and subtract two hours, that's what we always did with any assignation which could have been overheard by someone else. I wonder if they still use the old formula?'

'Oh, Lord, so unless we know what their delay factor is, we don't know when they are going to turn over the bank?'

'That is why it matters if Nina told you what Madame Stella said, or the corrected time.'

'We'll have to find Nina. And we'll have to rescue Dot.'

'Quite. I suggest that we wait until the middle of the night. Then we will be in a position to surprise them.'

'I don't want them surprised,' objected Phryne. 'I want to sneak in, remove Dot and Nina, and then sneak out without waking the guard. I want them to rob this bank and be caught. Bank robbery is a hanging offence. I want them to hang. They killed an innocent boy and he died in my arms and they have kidnapped my friend. The argument does not convince you, Peter?'

Peter shrugged. His eyes were shadowed black in the dimming light, 'So many innocent boys have died in my arms,' he said, sadly. 'I have long since stopped demanding that someone should avenge their deaths. There is not enough blood on the earth to wash out the offences committed. Let the dead one lie. He will not cry out from the ground.'

'He cries out upon me,' said Phryne fiercely, 'and if not I, then Nina shall avenge him. What shall we do until midnight?'

Peter Smith held out his arms. 'Come, Phryne, and let me comfort you as you comfort me,' he suggested. 'The flesh shall answer for blood.'

With a shiver that was not entirely lust, Phryne subsided into arms which had harboured dying men. Peter Smith found the anarchist tattoo on Phryne's breast and kissed it gently.

There were worse ways to spend the time, Phryne thought, as her tense muscles unlocked under his practised hands.

◇◇◇

After what seemed to be a journey of days, Dot was dragged out of the car and, still wrapped in the stifling blanket, forced to walk up two steps and into a house. She was shoved around a corner and into a space; she stumbled and fell to her knees.

Someone laughed. Dot stopped crying and tried to wipe her face.

'Stay there,' said a guttural male voice. 'Stay there until it is all over. Then you shall die, Miss Fisher!'

A door slammed. Dot fought her way out of the blanket, which had indeed been used for transporting engines, wiping the grease and tears from her eyes. She was in a small room in a house, with a window which had been boarded up. She was not alone. Huddled into a bundle in one corner was a figure with straggling red hair who was crying like a funeral. The room contained, otherwise, only a litter of boxes, a grindstone, and whole generations of spiders.

'Here, let me out!' yelled Dot. There was a laugh from the other side of the door, but no answer.

'Do not call,' said the red-headed girl, wearily. 'They will mistreat you if you make a noise.'

She unwound herself and sat up, revealing a face discoloured with bruises. She had lost two teeth.

'You aren't Miss Fisher,' said the girl through her split and puffy lips. 'Who are you?'

'Dot. I'm Miss Fisher's maid. Keep your voice down. If they think they've got Miss Phryne, so much the better. What's your name?'

'Nina Gardstein. Pleased to meet you.'

'Dot Williams, and I ain't altogether pleased to meet you. What's happening? Where are we? Why are they keeping us here? And who beat you up?'

'Too many questions. We are in Collingwood, in their house. They are keeping us safe until they do their bank robbery. Then they may just leave us here or they may kill us. Max and Karl beat me. Casimir held me while they did so because I was seen talking to Miss Fisher. They think I have told her about the robbery. And they are right, I have. So they were right to beat me. But if Bill finds out where I am, he may come and rescue me. I hope that he does not.'

'Why?'

Dot had her bearings and was replaiting her hair. This action always soothed her nerves.

'Because they will kill him. They have a Lewis gun.'

'What's that?'

Nina twitched a canvas cover from a large metal object. It looked disassembled.

'This is. We cannot use it. They have the magazine. It is just stored here, like we are stored.'

'I've still got my handbag,' said Dot, irrelevantly. 'I've got a comb and a purse and a lipstick and a compact and a nailfile and a book of stamps and…aha…some barley sugar. Is there water in that jug?'

'A little, and we don't know if we will get any more.'

'I'll just have a mouthful, then, and we'll eat these lollies. Then we'll think about how we are to get out.'

'Will Miss…will she be looking for you?'

'High and low,' said Dot confidently. 'She'll find me, I'd bet my life on it.'

'You are betting your life on it,' said Nina, and took some barley sugar.

Chapter Twelve

'Verily?
You put me off with limber vows, but I
Though you would seek to unsphere the stars
with oaths,
Should yet say, "Sir, no going." Verily,
You shall not go.'

William Shakespeare, *The Winter's Tale*

Phryne's head was pillowed on the naked and admirable chest of her favourite anarchist, when he roused her with another kiss.

'Mmm?'

'Your minions are here, madam, my love, and a very worried young policeman. Should you receive them as you are?' Phryne stretched, and Peter stroked the length of her pale body from shoulder to calf.

'You are so beautiful,' he said softly. 'Must you adventure this night? I and your wharfies can do this business. I could not bear it, Phryne, that having found you I should lose you to bullet or knife. These are dangerous men.'

'I am dangerous myself,' smiled Phryne, sitting up and kissing him. 'And I had better find some clothes. Besides, there is no need for you to come along,' she added, finding her underclothes. Peter Smith protested.

'But you do not know where the house is.'

'I bet that Bert and Cec do.'

'And I might be able to reason with them.'

'Do you really think so?'

Peter collapsed back into the embrace of Phryne's feather bed and groaned.

'It is true. They will not listen to me. Command me, *Generale*.' He pulled on his shirt. 'Give me my trousers and I shall obey your orders.'

'Good. Come down, then, and let's review the troops. What time is it?'

'Just after eleven by your clock.'

◇◇◇

Bert and Cec were drinking beer in the salon and Constable Collins was pacing from wall to wall, refusing to sit down even when offered a drink. They all looked up as Phryne descended, clad in black trousers and pullover and soft shoes.

'Tell me all,' she invited. 'You first, Constable.'

'Miss Fisher, since this is a private war perhaps you'd better call me Collins.'

'All right, Mr. Collins, you have been to the Latvian Club. What happened?'

'Nothing, Miss Fisher. It was innocent and rather fun. Lots of dancing and some very nice sausages and dark bread. Not what I've tasted before but nice. They all danced, blokes and girls, dressed in these costumes. I danced too. They started off and finished by singing "God Save the King." Nothing anyone could object to. Miss Williams would have like it…have you heard anything about…'

'Nothing. Do sit down, Mr. Collins! I can't think when anyone is pacing like a caged animal. We shall have things to do soon. I promise. Bert? Cec?'

'Two addresses, Miss. We was lucky. Met a bloke who knows a bloke who's a cane cutter and he's sweet on one of these anarchist sheilas. He knows where both houses are. One's in 'Wood and one's in St. Kilda, just around the corner. And we got another whisper. A bloke who knows some very nasty blokes reckons these anarchists have been buying guns and ammo.'

'Legally?' asked Phryne. Bert gave her a scornful smile.

'What do you think? .303 calibre, and lots of it. You know what that means.'

'No, what does it mean?'

'A machine-gun,' said Bert. 'No one wants that much .303. You'd have to shoot all the kangaroos in the country to use it up.'

'A Lewis gun, Bert?'

'Yair, could be.' Bert rolled a smoke. He had not encountered a Lewis gun for more than ten years, and did not altogether want to renew his acquaintance.

'Rate of fire?'

'Rapid,' said Cec. 'Five hundred rounds a minute. Forty-seven rounds per drum. Only weighs twenty-eight pounds. Two thousand yard, sighted. Fifty-and-a-half inches long.'

'Reliable?'

'Yair. Air cooled. "Another ten rounds and the water'll be hot enough for tea," that's what our sarge used to say about our Vickers. Air's better. They're pretty reliable. They were designed to cut down a row of men going over the top. And they used to, too.' Cec shut his eyes for a moment. 'Yair, they were effective all right. My oath they were.'

'We got trouble,' opined Bert. 'Big trouble.'

'We knew that. They won't want to unveil their Lewis in the suburbs. Even in Collingwood the neighbours are going to complain about a machine-gun. I suppose they want it for the bank job. I don't think that they'd dare to use it before that. In any case I am assuming that they will not, because they won't have time. Anyway where on earth did they get a Lewis gun?'

'Lots of things came back from the Great War, Miss. Lewis'll strip down and fit in a few kitbags. Someone may have wanted a souvenir. One of our mates brought a whole bicycle in from the Dardanelles. Everyone carried a bit and the rest went in the hold as "engine parts," Cec and me brought back pistols.' Bert glanced uneasily at Collins. Even out of uniform and about to engage on criminal enterprise, a cop was a cop. Collins stuck both fingers in his ears.

'So they could have a Lewis, easy. If they haven't, why are they buying up big on .303? .303 is for killing people, not rabbits.'

'Good point. All right. Now, I want Dot back. If you have to shoot a few of them to get her then don't let me stop you. I will go to the Collingwood address with Mr. Collins. Bert and Cec, you take St. Kilda. Peter, you stay here. The number of my favourite policeman, Jack Robinson, is next to the phone. If we aren't all back within two hours, call him. I'm leaving you here in case the house is attacked,' she added. 'You have two girls and Mr. and Mrs. Butler to protect. Don't fail me.'

'I will not fail you, *Generale*,' promised Peter, kissing Phryne's hand. 'You may repose your trust in me.'

'Oh, Bert,' added Phryne, 'if you find Nina Gardstein there, bring her along.'

She was watching Peter Smith, who flinched. A small flinch, but definite.

'Don't hurt her. I want to give her back to her cane cutter, who will get her out of the state. She might be next in line for the chop, having helped me.'

She was not mistaken. That was a wince. What was Nina Gardstein to Peter Smith?

That mystery, however, could wait. Bert and Cec went out into the night which was cool and damp but not cold. Spring appeared to have come in time to prevent house breakers from getting pneumonia.

'How did you come here, Mr. Collins?'

'I walked, Miss Fisher.'

'Then we shall take my car. I'll just go and have a word with Mr. Butler and then we shall be off.'

Mr. Collins and Peter Smith were left facing one another in the sea-green room. Peter took a seat and poured a glass of beer.

'She's a live wire, isn't she?' chuckled Collins, uneasily. 'Do you think she knows what she is doing?'

Peter Smith smiled angelically.

'If you repose your trust in anything, Mr. Collins, you can rely on her. She may whisk you into the night as on a broom and frighten the wits out of you, but what she swears to do, she will do. And she is very fond of her maid.'

'So am I,' confessed the young man, helplessly. 'If I get caught doing this then it's bang goes my career, but I don't care. I only hope Miss Williams and this anarchist sheila Nina are all right.'

'So do I, Mr. Collins. If I believed in any God, I would pray for her. For them.'

Phryne imparted her instructions to a calm Mr. Butler, promised that the war would be over soon and that after peace was declared they would live for months in uninterrupted tedium. Then she went to collect her fellow burglar.

'Right. Don't let anyone in, Peter. Except us, of course. And don't drink all the beer. We'll be back.'

Peter Smith kissed Phryne with sudden and unexpected passion, released her, and resumed his place by the fire.

◇◇◇

No one had come into the room, and Dot was thirsty, dusty, hungry, and needed to find a toilet.

'They haven't even given us a bucket,' she muttered. 'Nina, can you call and ask for some water and to let me go to the ladies?'

'To go where?'

Dot was embarrassed. She had learned the phrase in French. '*Je veux faire pipi*,' she explained.

'Oh, I see. I'll try. I'm so dry I mightn't be able to call. Comrades! Even in prison one gets bread and water,' she cried, her sibilants hissing through gapped teeth. 'And even animals are not asked to piss on the floor!'

Dot blushed. Nina listened.

'Someone's coming,' she said. She waited until the footsteps stopped and called, 'Bread and water, comrade, and a bucket, at least! Can we dig a hole in the floor?'

The door was flung open. Dot retreated under her blanket, was seized and marched out. Her guard seemed to want to cover her face, presumably so that she could not survey the anarchists' den. This suited Dot. She was conducted to a very dirty lavatory in the yard. Although her captor did not release her arm, she was hidden under the blanket and was able to forget about him sufficiently to make use of the facilities. She was shoved against a sink, where she washed her hands without soap and splashed her face, and then she was frog-marched back to the room. Nina was treated alike, and slapped, to judge by the sound, when she subjected her gaoler to a stream of abuse in some foreign tongue. Nina was brave, Dot reflected, but not cunning.

Nina was flung back into the cell and someone shoved after her a metal tray on which reposed a big jug of water and a loaf of sour bread. Nina tore this up and gave Dot half. It tasted odd and not at all like real bread but she forced herself to chew it and swallow calmly, sipping water in between mouthfuls.

◇◇◇

Phryne steered the Hispano-Suiza into Smith Street and stopped outside the nearest pub to the address she had been given.

'I'll leave the car here,' she explained to Collins. 'We walk. This is a tough place but not as tough as other places I have seen. Stand up, man, don't look so furtive. If you look like a victim, people will treat you like a victim. Look like you have a place to go and you can breeze through most things. Don't look anyone in the eye,' she added. 'It attracts the wrong kind of attention. There, see? There must be an SP down that lane. There's his cocky. And he hasn't moved. We pass muster as innocent bystanders. Come on. This is the house.'

It was a worker's cottage. The front windows were heavily curtained, and the letterbox in the door had been blocked. Weeds grew high in the front garden. While it did not actually have 'Den of Bolsheviks' painted on the front door, Phryne was sure that she was in the right place.

Parked in the street was a black Bentley with one tyre flopping from its rim.

'How do we get in?'

'"When dealing with suspicious folk, boldness is all,"' quoted Phryne. 'We bluff them. Have you got your badge?'

'Yes, Miss Fisher.'

'All right. You will be taking a risk that they don't shoot you through the door, but I don't think that they will. Go up and pound on it. When they come, this is what you do.'

◇◇◇

Dot was no longer hungry or thirsty, and the work she and Nina had been engaged upon had given her some exercise and broken two fingernails, the grindstone and her nailfile. No one had come near them since they had been fed, and it was getting late. There was no light at all from the boarded-up windows. Dot fished for her watch.

'Half-past ten. Do you want to try and sleep?'

'To what purpose? They have not turned off the light.' The bare electric bulb swung against the flaking ceiling.

'Simple,' said Dot, and threw her compact at it. The bulb smashed, the compact broke open, showering them with powder, and it was suddenly and blessedly dark.

'You are a good friend,' said Nina, lying down on half of Dot's blanket. 'Also a very resourceful comrade. Do you still think that Miss Fisher will come?'

'She'll come,' said Dot, and closed her eyes.

◇◇◇

Bert and Cec arrived at the Fitzroy Street address and decided on the simple approach.

'We kick down the door and start shooting if they resist,' said Bert.

'What about the hostages?' worried Cec.

'Better we get in quick than hang about scratching our arsebones in the snow,' argued Bert. 'Come on, Cec.'

The Fitzroy Street house was dark. Bert turned the handle. The door was open.

'See if you can find a light, mate,' urged Bert, after flicking the switch to no avail. Cec produced an electric torch.

'No one home, mate.'

They crept softly along the hall. Cec nudged Bert. There was a light in the kitchen.

Sitting by the kitchen table, a thin woman was praying. The room was empty apart from her. On the table were three icons of Byzantine saints, three candles and three photographs—a young man, a young woman with curly hair, and 'the Honourable Phryne Fisher at home' cut from a popular magazine. Bert and Cec stopped at the door.

'Come in,' said the woman, pushing back her black hair. 'If you have come to kill me, I welcome you.'

'We ain't come to kill you, Miss. We're looking for…for your anarchist mates,' faltered Bert.

'Collingwood,' said Maria Aliyena sadly. 'But she will be dead by now, your Miss Fisher. All dead, all dead—Yourka, Miss Fisher and poor Nina. Put out like candles. All dead,' she repeated.

All in all, it came as something of a relief when Bill Cooper the cane cutter came barrelling down the hall demanding his girl.

'Bert, Cec,' Bert introduced them. 'Who are you?'

'Bill Cooper. I'm looking for…'

'Your sheila. Nina. We know.'

'How…?'

'Come out of here, mate, it's like an undertakers. Nina ain't here, and neither is the…person we're looking for. Come on out of it,' said Bert, and sighed with relief when he had regained the street. The three men stood on the pavement to exchange information.

'They were going to kidnap Miss Fisher?' said Bill. 'Why?'

'Why have they locked up your girl?'

'Because she was speaking to Miss Fisher. Oh, I see. Now what do we do?'

'We go back to Miss Fisher's house and drink her beer and wait to see what happens. She's gone herself to 'Wood and she's wild enough at us already for not preventing the snatch, so I ain't gonna risk her going really crook. Come on, mate. Nothing more you can do here. And you don't want to get between Miss Phryne and what she wants to do.'

'Won't she need help?' asked the cane cutter. Bert laughed.

'She ain't never needed it while I've known her,' he said, sardonically. 'Come on, mate, you don't want to queer her pitch. She's a very bright lady indeed, is Miss Fisher. For a capitalist,' he added.

'What shall we do about her in there?'

'She ain't none of our business,' said Bert. 'Get a move on, eh? I'm perishing for a drink.'

Bill Cooper, bewildered, went quietly.

◇◇◇

'Are you sure that this'll work?' asked Collins. Phryne gave him a friendly push.

'Of course I'm not sure. Off you go. I'll try for a side window. Make a lot of noise and, if you can, get them all out of the house. Break a leg, Hugh.'

Phryne floated like a small black cloud over the fence, through the weeds, and down the side-way between two houses. She had a jemmy in her hand and was so silent that she jumped when Collins knocked his loud constabulary knock on the rickety front door.

'Come on, open up!' he said loudly. 'Police here!'

Phryne gritted her teeth, waiting for a fusillade of shots through the night, but no answer came.

As she passed the side window, she saw that it alone of the windows had been boarded neatly.

'Dot?' she whispered.

Dot had awoken as soon as she heard hammering on the door. She heard the whisper and was at the window in a moment.

'Miss Phryne?'

'Yes. Wedge your door and I'll rip off these boards. See what you can do about the inside.'

As quietly as she could, Phryne jemmied at the window. Fortunately the boards were not individually attached, the boarding being revealed as a pallet which had been carelessly nailed over the space. It dropped without much noise.

The anarchists had joined Collins at the door. He was sounding at his most official and pompous.

'If you'd like to step out here, sir, you will see that the back tyre has been punctured. Now we have had a lot of hooliganism in the area, and we are most concerned that honest citizens like yourselves...'

Phryne stifled a laugh and Dot managed to tear off the board covering the window latch and undid it, completing the ruin of her fingernails.

The raising of the window seemed to make more noise than the forging of a whole set of horseshoes. They stopped with held breath. Someone tried the door, found it locked, and the footsteps moved away.

'Now, Dot! Before your nice policeman runs out of arguments.' Phryne hauled, Dot wriggled, and she was out of the window and crouching in the cold sour grass. Nina, who was plumper, had to remove another board before she could push herself free. Phryne leaned the pallet back against the window. She had no way of reattaching it, so the anarchists would know that the escaping prisoners had received outside help. At the door, Constable Collins, sounding rather hoarse, was allowing his interlocutors to return to the house. He bade them a polite good night and paced away slowly as the door shut, locked, and bolted. He stopped by the car, then went on.

He had not gone three paces before an arm was slipped through his own and Dot smiled up at him. She was greasy and dusty and had evidently been crying a good deal lately but her eyes were shining.

'I said I'd go out with you tonight, didn't I?' she asked, and Hugh Collins felt his heart turn over. They were almost back to the pub, and the car, when lights went on in the house, and a howl went up. All four began to run.

'I didn't know it would be this exciting, though,' added Dot, and took Hugh's hand as they ran to the pub and piled into Miss Fisher's car.

'No hurry, Miss,' said Hugh Collins, comfortably. He put one arm around Dot's shoulders and produced something from his jacket pocket. Phryne saw it as she started the Hispano-Suiza and rolled decorously out into the road.

It was a rotor arm.

Chapter Thirteen

*'Liberté! O Liberté! Que de crimes on commet
en ton nom!'*
*(Liberty! O Liberty! What crimes are commit-
ted in thy name!)*

Madame Marie Roland,
from the scaffold, 1793

Jane and Ruth waited until the door had slammed for the last
time and Mr. and Mrs. Butler had retreated into their own
quarters before creeping, soft-footed, into Phryne's salon. There
they found Peter Smith, sitting calmly on the sofa with a pistol
within reach and a glass of beer in his hand.

'Mr. Smith, we can't sleep,' began Ruth.

'And since you're awake,' added Jane.

'Perhaps you would talk to us,' concluded Ruth. Peter Smith
smiled slowly.

'Come and sit next to me.' He indicated his couch. 'And I will
tell you a story. It will be a while before they all get home, and
waiting is nervous work. Quietly, now, girls. Have you slippers
and gowns? Phryne will not be pleased if you catch cold.'

Both girls whisked into their room and pulled on their dress-
ing-gowns of soft undyed wool and sheepskin slippers, though
the night was not cold.

'Tell us a story,' begged Jane, throwing herself down next to Phryne's lover. 'A place we have never been.'

Peter cast about for a story suitable for maidenly ears as they settled either side of him. Putting down his glass, he began to speak softly, so that they had to strain their ears to hear him.

'Once in Russia there was a witch called Baba Yaga. She lived in a hut on chicken's legs, enormous chicken's legs, so it could go anywhere. She rode through the sky in a storm in a pestle and mortar, grinding the heavens. A dreadful creature, Baba Yaga, conceived in hell, who ate her children—yes, Baba Yaga devoured all her children whole.'

Jane and Ruth looked at one another. They considered themselves too old for fairy stories but Peter Smith was no longer talking to them. Jane mouthed 'allegory,' a term which she had just learned. Ruth made a face at her.

'Once a young girl was sent out by her wicked stepmother to Baba Yaga's house to borrow a cup of flour. The stepmother wanted to get rid of the girl. Her name was Vasilissa. Her mother had died and her father had married again and her father's wife hated her, because she was pretty and skilled and the father loved her. So Vasilissa was sent through the dark wood, alone, where the trees strangle with vines and the floor of the wood is pit-falled with traps.'

Ruth was leaning against Peter from one side, Jane on the other. His voice was low, but perfectly clear, and he felt their listening warmth like two little fires beside him.

'Vasilissa got to Baba Yaga's house on its chicken's legs. The gate was made of the bones of men she had torn apart and eaten. The gateposts were topped with skulls and in them the shadow of eyes gleamed; the latch of the gate was of fingers, which writhed and knotted and would not let Vasilissa in. She was so frightened that she wanted to run away, then she heard a girl's voice sigh and say pitifully, "Oh, I am so lonely, so lonely!" She told the lock "Open" and it opened. She told the hut "Stand" and it stood still on its chicken's legs, each as big around as a tree. She commanded the door "Let me in" and the door let her in, for what can stand against the fearlessness of love?'

Ruth and Jane exchanged glances. They both thought of Phryne haring out to rescue Dot.

'In the hut was a young girl, and she cried, "Oh, my sister, my darling, I was so lonely without you! I will give you rest and food, but you must flee before my mother comes, or she will eat you up!"

'"Oh, my sister," said Vasilissa, "I have been sent to beg a little flour and I am so lonely in my stepmother's house!"

'"Come in," said Baba Yaga's daughter. "And we will think what is to be done."

'So the two girls sat down by the fire in the hut with chicken's legs, and they were very happy together. They sang and sewed and combed each other's hair, when suddenly the trees outside thrashed and cracked under the lash of a dreadful wind, and Baba Yaga returned. Quick as a flash, Baba Yaga's daughter turned Vasilissa into a needle and stuck her in the broom. "My darling, my daughter," said Baba Yaga, "why can I smell human blood?" "An old man came past, Mama, but I did not make him stay. He was too old and stringy and you would not have found him toothsome."

'Wait,' said Peter Smith, leaping to his feet. 'Was that a noise?'

He prowled out to the back door, pistol in hand, then returned and sat down again.

'No, nothing. Are you not tired, girls? Would you not like to go back to bed?' he asked, hopefully.

'No. Tell us the rest of the story. It's an allegory, isn't it?'

'Yes, it is an allegory,' agreed Peter, sounding suddenly tired. 'What of?'

Peter Smith did not answer and continued the story.

'Baba Yaga slept and went out and her daughter magicked Vasilissa out of the broom and they sat all day talking and knitting and combing their hair, until Baba Yaga returned and the trees whined under the weight of her mortar and pestle. "Why do I smell human bones, daughter?" asked Baba Yaga. "There were two men, Mother, foresters. I tried to make them stay, but they would not." "Next time set a trap for them," growled Baba Yaga, and slept. Then she went out, and her daughter retrieved Vasilissa from the broom and they sat all day by the fire, laughing and telling tales and drinking tea. They were so happy that this time they did not notice the branches snapping under Baba Yaga as she landed and flung open the door. "Daughter, darling daughter, what a morsel you have found for your mama. Into the oven with her!" "No," cried Baba Yaga's daughter, "this one you shall not eat," and she gave Baba Yaga such a push as sent her into her own oven, then the two girls snatched up their knitting and their brush and comb and ran into the forest, taking one of the skull gateposts to show the way. Baba Yaga screamed as she dragged herself out of the oven, and flew after them like winter.'

'Like winter?'

'Do you know anything more merciless than winter?'

Jane nodded. She had linked hands with Ruth across Peter. The story seemed to have some personal application for them.

'So Baba Yaga's daughter flung the hairbrush behind her, and it grew into a dense thicket tangled with blackberries. It took Baba Yaga an age to struggle through it, but she came on, and the girl flung the comb behind them. It grew up into a forest of tall trees, and Baba Yaga had to tear them up with her teeth; it took a long time, but the girls were tired, and their strength was failing. Terror is very draining. They had not got very far before they heard the witch gnaw through the last of the trees and Vasilissa threw back the long strip of knitting, which turned into a deep wet bog. Baba Yaga was a fire-witch. Into the bog she flung herself, eager for human blood, and in that bog she sank, first to her knees, and then her hips, to her waist, her shoulders, and at last the mouth with snake's venom drowned under the mud, and Baba Yaga was gone.'

'Ooh,' squeaked Jane. 'Poor witch!'

This had evidently not been the effect which the teller had expected. He gave Jane a startled look, then continued, 'The two girls came to the stepmother's house, and she demanded,

"Have you brought the flour?" and Vasilissa said, "No, but I have brought Baba Yaga's daughter and light." And the light from the skull's eyes burnt the stepmother to cinders. Baba Yaga's daughter and Vasilissa lived together in the house, combing each other's hair, singing, and knitting forever after.'

'Gosh! What a story. Thank you, Mr. Smith. Can I get you more beer? Do you think Miss Phryne will be all right?' Jane prattled. She knew that she was doing so, but the story had made her uneasy. Peter Smith smiled at her. Although he seemed like an old man to Jane, she could see why Miss Phryne liked him. The smile on his lined face was a child's smile, open and innocent and joyful. The effect was very endearing.

He had also instantly understood, without prompting, that Jane was frightened and babbling to cover up. Such intelligence, in Jane's experience, was not often to be found in the male sex.

Ruth refilled Peter's glass and asked, 'Are you Russian, Mr. Smith? That's a Russian story, isn't it?'

'Russian? No. I come from Latvia. It is on the shores of the Baltic. Do you know where that is?'

'Yes, we had it in Geography,' agreed Jane, knitting her brows. 'Let's see. With a warm water port, that's why Russia wants it, and the capital is…is…I've got it! Riga.'

'It is Riga.'

'What's it like, Latvia? Are there reindeer?'

'No, Ruth, that's Lapland,' corrected Jane.

'No reindeer, but trees. Dark forests of pine in the cold parts away from the sea; low forest of scrub on the shore, where I used to go with my brothers to pick up bits of amber from the tide line.' Peter smiled again. 'Are you not tired, ladies?'

'No,' they chorused. 'There is someone at the door!'

Peter Smith got to his feet, gun in hand. The doorbell rang. With a gesture, he ordered the girls back into their room and they went without a word. Peter Smith put on all the lights in the hall and outside and waited.

'Bert, Cec and Bill Cooper,' said a gruff voice. 'Let us in, mate, it's starting to rain.'

Peter Smith unlocked and unbolted the main door and allowed the three men to come in; then he bolted and locked the door again.

'How did it go?'

'Not there, mate, so she must be at the other address. Give a man a beer, Ruthie,' added Bert, who had sighted both girls lurking in their doorway. 'Nothing's happened yet. We come back to wait for Miss Phryne. What about you? All quiet?'

'All quiet,' said Peter. 'We have been telling fairy stories. No one has called. Was there anyone in the Fitzroy Street house?'

'Only some mad tart. Sitting at the kitchen table and crooning to herself. Off her rocker,' concluded Bert, suppressing what Maria had said about Phryne being dead. 'Thanks, Ruthie. You know the way to a man's heart.'

Ruth did not repeat what Phryne had said about this path, as she did not want to shock the company. Jane perceived that they were in the position of hostesses, and found another glass of beer for Cec, and one for this massive individual called Bill. He was huge. He made Jane feel like a baby in comparison, but he had a nice smile. He was worried and trying not to show it.

'You reckon Miss can get Nina out?'

'If anyone can do it, she can. O'course, we don't know what the resistance is like. Or whether they've limbered up their Lewis.'

'They should have sufficient ammunition for it,' said Peter. 'I don't, however, know how many drums they have managed to buy.'

'I heard three,' said Bert, sucking foam off his upper lip.

'Three'd be enough for a massacre,' said Cec.

They sat silent for several minutes. Peter, Cec and Bert all had very unpleasant memories of machine-guns.

Bill Cooper had never seen one. Where he came from, quarrels were settled with cane cutter's machete or fists.

'Never mind,' he said resolutely. 'Nothing we can do. How about a game of cards, eh? To pass the time.'

'Gotta do something,' said Bert. 'You know where the cards are, Ruthie?'

'No, but we've got some, I'll find them.'

'Poker?' asked Peter Smith. Bert looked at him.

'You play poker?'

'I have played,' said Peter, smiling the smile of the man who has made many transatlantic journeys.

'All right then. That's four. You want to play, girls?'

'You'll have to teach us,' warned Jane. 'We usually play pontoon.'

'Come on, then.' Bert took the cards, which were rather dog-eared, and counted them. 'All right. You sit next to Cec, Jane, and Ruthie can sit next to me, and we'll be jake.'

◇◇◇

Two hours later, when Phryne escorted Dot and Collins carrying Nina to the house, Jane had cleaned out her opponents to the tune of fourteen shillings seven pence and a kopeck, two drachmas and a trouser button, which was all that Peter Smith had in his pockets.

'Just a friendly game, Miss,' said Bert, staring at Jane as if he wondered where she had inherited her gambling luck. 'And little Janey here is a real shark. Any trouble, Miss?'

'Not really. We're a little battered, but still in one piece. Lay her down on the sofa, Hugh. She's all right, Bill,' she added, as the cane cutter gave a muted roar and fell to his knees beside Nina. 'They beat her, but it's not as bad as it looks.'

'Mongrel bastards! Oh, Nina love, I told you not to go back to them! What have them dogs done to you?'

'She'll shock you less when we get her cleaned up a bit. Bert, was there anyone in the other house?'

'Just a crazy woman, Miss. No one else. Not even the Lewis.'

'That's in the Collingwood house. Dot was locked up with it. What's your pleasure, Dorothy? You have done very well, very well indeed. My house is yours. What would you like first?'

'A cuppa tea.' Dot sank down into a chair. 'Hot. Then a bath. Hot. Oh, Miss, I was that scared!'

'But brave. If you are not scared then there is no merit in being brave. Oh, Dot, I thought I'd lost you!' Phryne embraced Dot, who was sitting dusty and smeared in the velvet chair with Hugh Collins' arm around her waist.

'Jane, run out to the kitchen and put the kettle on: try not to wake the Butlers, poor things, I don't think that they like adventure all that much. Ruth, run upstairs and put on a bath. Fling in some pine bath salts, they're on the dressing-table, and bring me the first-aid box on the way back. Peter, was there any trouble while we were away?'

'Not a sign of it.'

'He told us a fairy story,' said Jane, in passing. 'An allegory.'

'Did you, Peter? An allegory of what?'

'The Revolution,' said Peter. 'What else?'

'What else indeed?'

Phryne poured herself a glass of rather good champagne, although only Peter showed a taste for it, which meant that she would have to drink half a bottle herself. She surveyed the hands of cards, laid down when she came in, and observed that Jane was about to make a Royal Flush. The child had a gift for gambling. Phryne picked up the King of Spades and felt a certain roughness on the back, where a thumbnail had marked it. The Queen of Spades was also marked. She caught Jane's eye as that young woman descended the stairs with the first-aid box and smiled meaningfully. Jane blushed.

'Ruth and me were reading a book about cardsharps,' she whispered, 'so we marked the whole deck. We didn't mean to cheat,' she pleaded, and Phryne patted her.

'If you could take in Bert, Cec and Peter with them, pet, then they were well done, and I don't think that we need to worry. But you had better give back their money.'

'Of course,' said Jane. She had already divided the pile of coins into stacks according to donor. Phryne took the first-aid box as Jane made a circuit of the room.

'We weren't playing for keeps,' she explained. They nodded solemnly, though Peter insisted that she keep a kopeck, drachma, and button.

Nina's injuries were, as Phryne suggested, less bad than they looked. When the young woman had washed her face Phryne applied iodine and plaster and Nina smiled painfully at Bill.

'Don't you see, I can leave them now,' she said, defiantly. 'I have not broken my word. They have flung me out. They will not even chase me, now. I do not like to run away,' she added. 'I am not much hurt and it is nothing if I should have secured my husband.'

She said this while vanishing into Bill Cooper's massive embrace, so the finer points of her discourse were lost.

Dot floated upstairs in a haze, compounded of relief and exhaustion in equal shares, and stripped off her clothes, which had not borne the night's entertainment well. She threw down her split stockings and damaged shoes, then laid aside her suit coat with the torn shoulder seams, her dusty skirt smeared with oil, and her shirt soaked in sweat. The water was hot and scented. She sank into it, biting back a cry as the water invaded the cuts on her hands. It had been in a good cause, she thought, and reached for the soap. Phryne's favourite scent, Nuit d'Amour. Night of Love. Dot thought of Hugh Collins and began to laugh helplessly, until she hiccupped and sank down to extinguish her rising hysteria in the foam.

Bill Cooper had been induced to try champagne, but declared it was a sour and fizzy wine and he preferred beer. Peter Smith sat quietly on the end of the sofa and Nina explained about the robbery.

'The time and place I gave you for the robbery were...corrected time. It will take place tomorrow at two. These are fierce men who will stop at nothing, and have no interest in human life, so they will not mind killing or dying. I would like some wine.'

Bill supplied champagne in a beer glass to his intended and glowed all over his big, ugly face. His paw held Nina's hand as gently as if he were holding a butterfly. Phryne replenished her glass. Jane and Ruth were having their first taste of champagne, which they had heard was the best wine in the world, and were not liking it much.

'It's sour,' complained Ruth to Jane, very quietly. Jane sipped at her glass, made a face, and then swallowed it down.

'It's all right if you gulp it,' she advised, and Ruth gulped. Both girls then became so sleepy that they did not protest when Phryne sent them to bed.

Dot came down the stairs wearing Phryne's lounging robe and silver slippers and had the satisfaction of stopping Hugh Collins in mid-sentence. He was arguing for a police presence at the robbery.

'Not many men, Miss Fisher, maybe a sharp-shooter…or…' He dried up. Phryne looked in the direction of his gaze and saw Dot, her wet hair trailing, feeling her way carefully down as though she was half-blind with exhaustion. She shone like the moon. Phryne looked on the gaffed-cod expression of the young policeman with interest. She had often produced that effect herself. It was interesting to see someone else do it.

Dot managed to get to the foot of the stairs and stood with one hand on the newel post, uncertain as to her balance.

'Oh, Dot!' cried Hugh Collins, and crossed the room to take her hand. 'You're worn out, girl dear. You should go to bed.'

'I just came to thank everyone for rescuing me,' said Dot, scanning the room and smiling at Phryne and the men. 'Thank you.' She turned and accepted Hugh Collins' escort up the stairs again, leaning heavily on his muscular arm. Phryne was pleased to see that constabulary instinct was so submerged that he did not even attempt to put a 'come-along-'o-me' grip on Dot.

Reaching her door, Dot kissed her suitor politely on the cheek, failed to co-ordinate her thoughts sufficiently to find a nightgown, fell down into her bed in the jade-and-silver gown and was asleep before her head found the pillow.

'Well, gentlemen, find yourselves a couch somewhere. Perhaps Nina would prefer my room?'

It appeared that Nina was not intending to move and anyway, she did not wish to leave Bill. Bill blushed and lay down on the floor next to the sofa. Bert and Cec took their leave, and Phryne held out her hand to Peter.

They passed Hugh Collins on the stairs.

'Two sharp-shooters, if you can get them,' smiled Phryne. 'No more, or you might scare them off. Telephone me tomorrow—oh, it's today, isn't it?—at about ten and tell me what you have been able to arrange. Give your sergeant my best regards. Good night.'

Hugh took his leave of the sleepers. Bert and Cec took him home to his blameless cottage in Footscray and his incandescent mother, who had been waiting up for him. He did not seem to be listening to her excellent discourse on thankless sons who kept their innocent mothers up all night—look at the time!—mothers who had wasted the best years of their lives bringing up shameless kids who didn't care for them at all. At this point Hugh Collins had got up from the kitchen chair on which he had been sitting and said, 'I'm going to bed. Good night, Mum,' and had kissed her politely on the cheek. She then realized that she had lost her ascendency, snapped, 'Who is she?' and received such a vague and delighted smile in return that she was quite quenched. She took herself off to bed without another word.

◇◇◇

Phryne smiled at Peter Smith.

'Stay with me?' she asked. He cupped her face in his big hand and stared into her eyes.

'Oh, Phryne,' he said softly. 'I would like to stay with you forever. I would like to close the door and never open it again.'

'That could be inconvenient.' Phryne did not like terms like 'forever.' 'You have to come out sometime.'

'Yes, you have to come out sometime. But not yet. This night, at least, you are mine.'

'I am,' agreed Phryne, and, leading him into her boudoir, shut out the other sleepers in the house.

Chapter Fourteen

'There is a tide in the affairs of men
That taken at the flood, leads on to fortune.
Omitted, all the current of their life
Is spent in shallows and in miseries.'
William Shakespeare, *Julius Caesar*

Phryne spent most of the night which remained in making love
to Peter Smith. He was as gentle, strong and responsive as ever—
more, if anything, as though some driving passion possessed him.
She got up to wash at four of the morning, and on her return
found that he was standing at the window, staring out to sea.
Little dots of light, which were ships, moved and converged on
the black velvet of the ocean.

'I will have to leave,' he said. 'After this is all done, and they
are caught, I will be marked, even by the old comrades who
remember…who remember the old days. I will lose you, Phryne,
just when I have found you. I do not know how I will bear it.'

'Where shall you go?' Phryne joined him at the window,
caressing the muscular swell of his shoulders. He kissed her hand.

'Another country, I fear,' he said. 'South America, maybe,
they will not look for me there. Perhaps I shall go to the back
country in Queensland with my daughter.'

'Nina is your daughter?'

'I have no secrets from you. Her mother died three years ago. She came here with me from Paris. A long, long time ago. Come now, Phryne, you are not jealous of a dead woman?'

Phryne smiled. She had never been jealous of anyone's lovers in her life.

'No, I was frowning for quite another reason. I shall miss you.'

'I do not know how I can leave you.'

'But you must find a way. I would not have you demonstrate your fidelity by getting murdered.'

'It could come to that. Nina was safe as long as I was held in respect, but they locked her up, and beat her. Our immunity is gone.'

'Never mind, Peter. We have tonight, or what is left of it, and perhaps we may meet again. In another country.'

'In another life,' agreed Peter. 'Come back to my arms. They will be empty enough without you.'

◇◇◇

Nine o'clock brought breakfast—of which Peter ate heartily— and a demand for a council from the girls, the Butlers and Dot. Phryne felt unequal to this but came down anyway.

Her audience was seated at the dining table. Dot was pale, head-achey and disinclined for conversation. Mr. and Mrs. Butler were worried. The girls were excited.

'It is like this,' Phryne began abruptly. 'I am attending a bank robbery, and no one is going with me. After today I solemnly promise to confine myself to paid and quiet cases within the law and not to ever get involved with revolutionaries again. Cross my heart. If you will bear with me for one more day, I expect peace, perfect peace, and no more people littering your floor. I shall ask Nina and Bill to stay here, and to promise not to leave the house until I give permission.'

Bill Cooper and Nina promised.

'Dot, Ruth, Jane, the same. I can't do this if any of you are in danger. Do you understand?'

They nodded, Dot appearing to regret the movement.

'Mr. and Mrs. Butler, if you will put up with this for one more day, I would be obliged, and naturally some token of my appreciation will appear in the monthly envelope. You have been much tried.'

Mrs. Butler, who was worried by Phryne's taut voice, said soothingly, 'It ain't been no trouble, really, Miss. We'll stay in.'

'Good. Now, everyone go and find something to do, except Dot, who is going back to bed. Perhaps you could take her up, Mrs. B. Girls, go and see her settled, there's aspirin in my dressing-table drawer. Go on, Dorothy, you can't go about being a hero and not suffer a hangover.'

Dot allowed herself to be led away. Bill Cooper and Nina got out the girls' marked cards. Mr. Butler went to answer the phone.

'Constable Collins, Miss Fisher,' he announced, and went off to give the silver the polishing of a lifetime.

Phryne took the phone. The young man sounded distressed.

'Miss Fisher, I can't get my boss to listen. He's given me leave to be there and to carry a pistol—he's even issued me one—but he won't believe that there will be a robbery. I can't shift him.'

'Never mind, Hugh. We can handle this—I hope. What calibre?'

'A .45. Miss Fisher, what are you going to do?'

'I'm not sure. Meet me at the bank at one-thirty. On the steps.'

'All right,' agreed the constable, and hung up.

'Peter,' she said imperiously, holding out her hand. 'Give me your gun.'

'My gun, Phryne?'

'Yes.'

'Why do you want it?'

'I have a good reason.' Peter produced a pistol. Phryne broke it, spun the action, counted the rounds, and snapped it back together.

'Excellent,' she approved. 'Nice and clean. I suppose I shouldn't ask where on earth you got a Colt .45?'

'No, you shouldn't.' Peter Smith was looking very uneasy. 'What are you going to do?'

'I don't know. For the moment, I am going back to my room to sleep for three hours. Are you coming?'

Peter Smith followed in her wake.

True to her word, Phryne slept until twelve, woke bedraggled and sad, having had bad dreams, and took a long bath. Her anarchist mark had faded away. She put on her street clothes, choosing a relatively wide skirt in case she had to run, and low-heeled shoes. Her costume was dark-blue and her hat sober and close-fitting. Elegant enough for the city, but not flamboyant. She did not want to attract notice.

Peter Smith said not a word as she kissed him lovingly and walked out of the house to her car, which she started with a mighty roar.

Peter Smith waited ten minutes, then opened the front door.

'Miss Fisher would not like you to go out, sir,' said Mr. Butler. 'Please reconsider.'

'I did not promise,' Peter reminded him. 'She did not ask me to promise. Say goodbye to the girls for me, and remind them of Baba Yaga's daughter.'

He slipped out into the street, and heard Mr. Butler lock the door behind him. He pulled his old felt hat down over his eyes and caught a tram to the city.

◇◇◇

Hugh Collins was not altogether pleased to see Miss Fisher on the steps of the imposing bank, although he wanted news of Dot. The small face under the cloche hat was set and he did not like either the glitter of her green eyes or the suggestive bulge at her waist.

'Miss Fisher, what are you going to do?' he asked again, and Phryne patted his arm.

'Come along, Constable, we are going to earn you a medal. Your boss hasn't relented, then?'

'No, Miss Fisher. How is Miss Williams?'

'I've sent her back to bed. Just reaction. She isn't used to adventure. And a good thing, too. One adventuress is sufficient for most households. Now, they have this machine-gun, and your task is to get the gunner. I don't know how they are going to bring it in. It might be anything. According to Cec, the whole thing is only about four feet long, and it only weighs twenty-eight pounds. Keep your eye peeled for it. This is the only entrance to the bank, they will have to come up here. I know all of them, and they won't have been able to travel far. Have you still got the Bentley's rotor arm in your pocket?'

'No, Miss Fisher.'

'Call me Phryne. Now, stay here. Look unofficial. The Lewis fires from a drum with forty-seven cartridges, so we have to stop them before they start firing or there will be hell to pay.'

Constable Collins watched the well-dressed people of Melbourne passing and re-passing him on the bank steps. He wondered how they would feel if they had known that an anarchist outrage was about to be enacted before their eyes. He envisaged the steps slippery with blood and screams echoed in his ears. He was so involved in this horrific vision that he jumped when Phryne handed him a bunch of spring flowers, bought from a barrow.

'Look at your watch every ten minutes,' she advised.

Constable Collins was the recipient of many pitying glances as he stood on the bank steps waiting for a girl who would never come. He saw Phryne as she crossed the banking chamber, chatted with a clerk, walked back, stopped to beg a light from a shocked city gent who did not approve of ladies smoking in public, strolled back to the counter for another word with the clerk, evidently an acquaintance.

Phryne made a small and significant gesture at Collins as three men stopped at the foot of the steps. One was carrying a roll of pretty blue wallpaper. It seemed very heavy. They began to mount the steps, and by the time they had reached Collins, one had begun to rip off the paper. The policeman sighted cold gun-metal beneath.

Hugh thrust his bunch of daffodils into a girl's hands and dived for Casimir, who struggled and shouted oaths. The two others turned back at the door and drew guns. The girl to whom Hugh had given the flowers clutched them and ran. Several people screamed.

They drew a bead on the struggling mass of Collins, the Lewis gun, and the drum of ammunition which Casimir was striving to fix on the Lewis. Casimir was as strong as an ox. One shot whizzed past Hugh's ear and clipped a shard off the bank's decorative stonework. Inside the bank, Phryne screamed, 'Everyone get down,' and ran for the door.

A loud voice saved Hugh Collins' life. There was another person in the bank who distracted the attention of Karl and Max.

'Traitors!' Peter's voice boomed in the vaulted chamber. 'You have betrayed the Revolution!'

Both of the anarchists were good looking young men, but their faces were as cold as masks, as empty of purpose now as of pity. Hugh and Casimir stopped fighting, remaining in their positions, with Hugh grabbing for the gun and Casimir locking the lever which fixed the drum.

'I have fought for the freedom of Latvia all my life,' continued Peter, his voice carrying as he moved forward into the light. 'I have given to it all I had to give. And you bring *illégalisme* to this peaceful place! Dogs, and sons of dogs! I denounce you. Give me your guns. Give them to me.'

'Your time is over,' hissed Karl, and they fired together. Peter Smith collapsed quietly, all the people in the bank shrieked, and in the confusion no one noticed two more shots. First Karl, and then Max fell slowly backwards down the steps into the respectable street, dislodging Hugh from Casimir, who finally managed to find the trigger of the Lewis among the torn paper.

As Phryne launched herself forward into his line of fire, he pulled the trigger and held it there.

The Lewis did not fire.

Hugh Collins disentangled himself from the dead Karl and the dying Max and seized Casimir in an unbreakable grip. He marched him up the steps, slipping in blood like paint, and found Phryne embracing Peter Smith as he lay on the tiled floor.

◇◇◇

The ambulance had gone, the bank's cleaners were mopping the entrance and demanding double pay for having to deal with blood, and Constable Collins was being cross-examined by a superior who was somewhat mortified and partly pleased, but determined not to show either emotion.

'So it was the good oil, was it?' he asked, moving his feet so that a disgusted cleaner could mop around him. 'Those commos told Miss Fisher the truth. Where is Miss Fisher, then?'

'She's gone in the ambulance with the bodies.'

'Morbid tastes for a young woman. Did you have to shoot both of them, Collins?'

'Yes, sir.' Collins stood up straight and handed over his revolver. 'Only two shots gone. They had shot an innocent bystander and they had the Lewis as well, sir.' He dropped the shells into his superior's hand.

'Oh, I'm not arguing, Collins.' He broke the gun, took a small sniff at the barrel, and stared at his constable. 'You know, those new smokeless cartridges are very good. I'd swear this gun hadn't been fired.'

'Very good ammunition, sir.'

'And I suppose that when the police surgeon digs the bullets out of them two dead'uns they'll be .45?'

'Yes, sir. Certainly, sir.'

'Well, it was lucky that you happened to be here, and with a gun as well. The press are going to love it. Bank robbery foiled by courageous constable. Well, the super'll be pleased. Just don't get above yourself, Collins!'

'No, sir.'

'And consider yourself lucky I don't ask you to turn out your pockets!' snarled the detective.

Hugh grinned. The two unused cartridges were buried in the bank's window box. He had thought about his pockets.

He walked down the newly cleansed steps to meet a covey of excited reporters, and wondered about the nature of fame.

◇◇◇

For the second time in what seemed like days, Phryne returned to her house soaked in blood, but this time she avoided notice. She stripped in her own room, stuffed the soiled clothes in the laundry basket, and hid Peter's gun under her mattress before she scoured her body clean. She took a large dose of chloral hydrate and, wrapped in her green coverlet, slept heavily for ten hours. She did not dream, but whimpered in her sleep.

◇◇◇

She woke to the noise of music. There were many voices and what seemed to be a party. Phryne could never resist a party. She flexed and stretched and found that she was supple. Half-term was over. Tomorrow Ruth and Jane would be going back to school, Nina and Bill Cooper to Queensland, Max and Karl would be in hell by now, and Peter…what of Peter? His ultimate destination was a mystery. Phryne made up her face with precise licks of the compact, pencilled in her eyebrows, and pulled on an Erté dress. What was happening downstairs?

She descended to find Nina and Bill dancing, Hugh holding Dot closer than even a foxtrot warranted, Jane and Ruth working the phonograph, and a man dressed, it seemed, mostly in bandages sitting on the sea-green sofa with a glass of the good champagne in his large, scarred hand.

Peter Smith looked up as Phryne swooped like a Valkyrie down the stairs and threw herself at him.

'They told me you were dead! Peter, they said that…'

'Ah, so they thought. But those dogs had so little skill that one bullet missed me altogether and the other made a neat hole in my shoulder.'

'But you were covered in blood! *I* was covered in blood!' Phryne began to laugh, and sat down on the floor. 'Peter, you fraud.'

'The morgue were most surprised to find that I was still breathing, for a ricochet had cut my forehead and I bled like a pig—as you noticed, sweet Phryne—and I must have looked dead. I frightened one attendant so badly that he fainted. The hospital say that the damage is small. They wanted to keep me, but I would not stay.'

He gathered Phryne into his embrace and whispered, 'They told me what you did. Two shots, and both to the heart. You have done a great thing for the Revolution.'

'I didn't do it for the bloody Revolution!' exclaimed Phryne. 'I did it because I thought that they had killed you. Reflex. I had my finger on the trigger and—I fired when they fired.'

'In any case, the Revolution is served. Have some wine.'

Phryne poured herself a glass of champagne. The phonograph was wound by Jane and the tinny voices chanted.

'It ain't gonna rain no more, no more,
it ain't gonna rain no more!
How in the heck can I wash my neck,
if it ain't gonna rain no more?'

The whole world, Phryne thought, sipping her wine and light-headed with relief, had gone suddenly and irretrievably mad.

Then Phryne remembered something and exclaimed from her seat on the floor, where she was resting her head on Peter's mistreated chest. 'What about the Lewis? Hugh, we could have been ruined, if the Lewis hadn't jammed. It was a miracle.'

Hugh beamed with honest pride and pulled Dot forward.

'Here's your miracle, Miss Fisher. Tell her, Dot!'

'Me and Nina were locked up with the gun, and we couldn't get out, so we had a look at it. We couldn't just steal some bits because they'd notice when they come to put it together again. Then we looked at it some more and I noticed that there was this long bit of pipe which had a pin at the top, and you could see that it was meant to slide up and down to reload the gun and to throw out the bullet, and there it was, see, and I still had my handbag, which had a nailfile, to undo the screws, and there was this grindstone, and we thought that we might be able to damage it, or bend it, p'raps, but we couldn't because it's hard metal, so we…'

'Filed it down? Dot, you're a genius.'

'I used to go shooting with my dad.' Dot blushed at this unmaidenly skill. 'I've seen guns before.'

'Marvellous,' commented Peter Smith.

Dot drew away, then said, 'Miss, Hugh's been in all the papers. His boss says that he's in line for a medal.'

'I told you so, Hugh.'

'But it was all you, Miss! It ain't fair!'

'I don't want to be in the papers, Dot. Let Hugh have his fame. He was very brave, anyway. I presume that he didn't know that the Lewis wouldn't fire?'

'No, Miss, I forgot to tell him.'

'Well, then, if any man deserves a medal, your Constable Hugh does.'

Phryne snuggled into Peter's good arm and asked, 'When are you going away?'

'Tomorrow, with Nina and Bill.'

'Sleep with me tonight, is it tonight?'

'Yes, it's early morning, now.'

'Come up, then. We haven't much time.'

◇◇◇

Farewells occupied most of Phryne's day. Nina had to be equipped for her journey. She collected her goods from the Fitzroy Street house. Maria Aliyena had gone. Phryne rummaged to some effect to find her clothes and goods to astonish the outback. Bill Cooper had a modest suitcase and Peter Smith had one bundle which contained all that he had managed to acquire in a lifetime's wandering.

Jane and Ruth, protesting that school would seem awfully flat after the excitement, were sent back to school with a hamper of cakes and amazing stories that they could not tell. Jane ran back from the car.

'Miss Phryne, Mary Tachell told me to tell you that she told her mother all about what was in Alicia's diary. Goodbye,' added Jane, kissing Phryne affectionately, and ran back to the car.

The harvest of this piece of news was gathered an hour later, when Dot and Phryne were dressing a giggling Nina in one of her new costumes, a pale yellow which had not suited Dot.

'Mr. Waddington-Forsythe on the phone, Miss Fisher,' intoned Mr. Butler, and Phryne bit her lip.

'Miss Fisher? I have to thank you for finding my daughter. Now my son has run away, leaving a letter in which he makes the most outrageous accusations about my wife. Will you take the case?'

Phryne struggled for adequate words, failed to find any, and let the phone drop back onto the hook.

'Mr. Butler, if that appalling man rings back, tell him I am not taking any cases at present. In future, Mr. Butler, I shall *never* be at home to Mr. Waddington-Forsythe!'

Mr. Butler picked up the telephone as it rang again and Phryne left him to it.

The Waddington-Forsythes were finished, socially. Mrs. Tachell could not possibly keep such juicy news to herself, thought Phryne, and returned to hook Nina into a green Chanel travelling dress while presiding over the destruction, in the garden incinerator, of her revolutionary garb.

They were at the door. Phryne took a deep breath, kissed Nina, shook hands with Bill Cooper. Then she turned to Peter, who was wearing the same shabby suit in which she had first seen him.

'Peter, will you take nothing?'

'Memories,' he said softly. 'I will remember you for all of my life.'

Without another word he walked down the steps and the others followed. They climbed into the big car and it pulled away into the traffic. They were gone, Phryne realized, shutting the door, all her visitors were gone. The house was empty, fine and cool; full of space.

She picked up the telephone and asked for a university college.
'Lindsay?'

A young voice answered.

'It's Phryne. Come out tonight?'

The telephone made a quacking noise.

'You can study Trusts some other time.'

The telephone seemed to agree. It asked a question.

'What is up? I've come through fire and death, Lindsay, my old dear, and I want to go dancing.'